REVERSE ABDUCTION

AN ALIEN ABDUCTION STORY

EVE LANGLAIS

PROLOGUE

"I WANT TO GO TOO!" Azteriya held up her arms to her father, a tall male with a fierce unsmiling countenance and hair as white as a new-fallen snow—before blood stained it.

"The mission I've been commissioned for will have much danger," he stated.

"I'm not afraid." She didn't understand the word fear. She brandished her dagger—the one specially crafted and gifted by her father—and snarled. "I will gut our enemies and take everything they own as my prize."

A touch of dust might have stung her father's bright gaze. "I believe you would." Father held out his hand, a big hand callused by battle and training. "Join me, daughter, and together we shall make our foes tremble with our combined might."

Pride swelled within Azteriya that her father, the most accomplished warrior in the galaxy, nay, the universe, was ready to grant a spot in his mercenary squad to his only daughter.

She took a step forward reaching for father's invitation—

A hand clapped down on her shoulder, heavier than the stone blocks used to sink those that ran afoul of Aressotle laws.

The shining gem of adventure was crushed as a dreaded voice interfered. "Where do you think you're going?"

Despite knowing the futility, Azteriya replied. "I am going on a mission with Father."

The grip on her shoulder tightened. Mother's voice emerged quite flat and firm. "You will do no such thing. It is a female's place to remain at home and nurture the hearth while the male hunts and gathers." Also known as raiding other planets and taking their goods.

As for nurture...the thought of having babies made Azteriya's nose wrinkle. "I don't want a baby." Ever.

"It is your duty."

"I don't want to," she stubbornly insisted. "I want to be a mercenary like Father." And his father before him.

From a young age, he'd taught her how to fight. Father didn't care it wasn't usually done. He'd trained her as ferociously as a son. Except now that Azteriya had reached the age other males went off to fight, she wasn't allowed because she lacked dangling bits between her legs. So unfair.

Words unwittingly spoken aloud.

"Unfair?" Mother's icy blue gaze fixed her. Pinned her like a bug before it got swept into the cooling unit for use later in a meal.

"Yes, unfair. There are societies that allow their females equal opportunities."

Mother's face twisted as if she'd sucked something very sour. And putrid. "Have you been reading the forbidden tomes again?"

The very tone of the query had Azteriya rolling her eyes. "Only you forbade them." The books were freely available in the resource centers of their city. "There is nothing wrong with learning about the cultures on other worlds."

Mother sniffed. "It is when they've lost all sense of decorum and let their females run about wildly doing whatever they please."

How was that a crime? "It's called equal rights, Mother. Some of them even had wars." An unenlightened planet in the far reaches known as Earth had even progressed enough that their females burned their mammary harnesses in protest.

Father attempted to intervene. "Our daughter is correct. Other cultures welcome their females among their fighting ranks."

The remark drew the laser glare his way. "Do not use barbarian cultures as an example. We are more evolved than them."

"Are we?" Azteriya couldn't help but taunt. "Or is it us who have yet to progress with the times?"

"You are insolent."

"No, I'm educated and not mentally deficient. I want to be a warrior."

"Never!" spat Mother. "Bad enough you insisted on dressing like a male, with your trousers and weapons. Going off to be a fighter? You would bring shame on this family."

"What shame?" Father asked. "We have a daughter

who is capable and strong. Did you know she can take down a bizzonn on her own now? Just like the males her age."

"But she's not a male. The rules are different for her."

"They shouldn't be. It's not fair," Azteriya said with a pout of her lower lip. "I hate wearing skirts and being proper."

"Insolence." Mother's fingers dug deep into her flesh. "This is your fault." Aimed at her father. "You and your stories not meant for delicate feminine ears. You will cease encouraging these flights of fancy." Mother didn't add a threat. Never noticed the hypocrisy that while she advocated females cater to their males, when it came to their home, Mother ruled the nest.

And Father obeyed, which meant the conversation about Azteriya joining him ended, but that didn't get rid of the dream. It became the start of her attempts to leave. Attempts that failed, but Azteriya never stopped trying.

One day I will roam the galaxy and show Mother, show all of them, that I am a mercenary like my father.

ONE

MANY GALACTIC ROTATIONS later (which for the humans reading stands for years)...

EXPRESSION CREASED IN CONCERN, Dorrys addressed Azteriya. "Are you sure you want to do this?"

"Very sure. Mother brought around three suitors to weigh my worth as a mate," Azteriya muttered. All of the male warriors born of acceptable families. Each one of them holding the opinion that a female's only worth existed in her ability to birth and cook.

"Three?" Dorrys sounded impressed. "How many does that make now that she's paraded you in front of?"

"Too many." Spoken in a grumble. "She's threatened to find even more if I don't choose soon." The fact that none of them appealed didn't dampen her mother's zeal in the least. She kept persisting in the erroneous train of thought that eventually Azteriya would meet the one that made her forget all her dreams.

Not likely. What she wanted couldn't be found on Aressotle. Hence why she'd hatched her latest plan to escape.

This time I won't fail. Azteriya leaned against the large shipping container behind which she and her closest friend hid. The busy hangar, situated planet side for intergalactic vessels retrieving local goods, didn't have many spots to conceal them in. If they were caught... someone would call Mother, and that wouldn't bode well for Azteriya.

A moue pulled at Dorrys' lips. "At least your mother is proactive about finding you a mate. Mine keeps telling me to shorten my hems and flirt more."

Azteriya snickered "On account you're the seventh daughter. She's worn out from all the mating feasts she's had to throw for your sisters." Said teasingly, and yet Azteriya envied her friend. Being an only child put a lot of pressure on Azteriya. It would be up to her to continue her family's line, to birth the next generation so their name didn't die out. Something her mother repeated over and over. Azteriya's reply of, "If you just want me to get impregnated, then why don't I visit the clinic for a fertilization injection?" didn't go over well.

Dorrys worried her lower lip. "This is a bad idea. If you must leave our world, then at least get your father to take you."

"I tried." Tried talking and arguing. Even resorted to weak tears. Her father resisted all emotional outbursts and logic.

As to her attempts to stow away? Each time Father found her and, with a shake of his head, said, "Your mother would kill me."

Probably very accurate. Mother might look genteel on the outside, but she could wield a knife and kill with a single stroke. Azteriya had seen it! Mother eschewed the local butcher, preferring the meals she made to be fresh.

Dorrys still argued. "What if this commander tosses you out of an airlock when he finds you aboard his ship?"

"He won't." Azteriya had watched the big armored fellow, at least fifteen handspans tall and yet not overly rough with those he dealt with. Just big.

"Are you sure you can even survive on board? What about breathing? Or food? What if nothing on his ship is compatible?"

Dorrys referred to the fact the commander wore a helm with a breathing apparatus, odd considering the logs Azteriya had accessed showed a gas ratio on his ship that she could breathe.

"I'll be fine. He's got a culinary unit on board."

"What if he tries to defile you? Have you seen the size of him?" Her friend looked genuinely concerned.

That caused her to smile. Azteriya patted her hip. "If he tries, I'll gut him and take over his ship."

"What if he kills you instead?"

Then she wasn't the warrior her father had raised. "I'll take that risk. Or would you rather see me sunken in the sea of tears?" Convicted of gutting the mate her mother kept trying to foist on her.

"Or you could just accept your fate." The moment she said it, Dorrys bit her lip. "What am I saying? Of course you won't. I wish I had your courage."

"Since when do you want to travel the stars and fight?"

Dorrys shook her head. "I meant to boldly find what I

need in life. I've all but given up hope of finding a mate here."

"The perfect male is out there for you."

A heavy sigh left her friend. "I wish I believed that. I'll miss you."

"As will I, dear friend." Azteriya clapped Dorrys on the arms, giving them a squeeze. "I'll try and message you when I can. But don't expect them too often. I shall probably be very busy having grand adventures."

"A part of me, a small part," Dorrys quickly added, "almost wishes I was going with you."

"Then come."

Her friend shook her head. "Unlike you, I can't fight, nor do I want to. But if you find a warrior out there who needs a mate, give him my coordinates."

"I promise that if I find a suitable one, I'll drag him back." Maybe she'd drag back a pair and stop her mother's complaints. A male that would stay at home and take care of the babies while she went off and pillaged the galaxy.

Excitement hummed inside her at the thought of finally achieving her dream.

A peek around the corner of the container had Dorrys squeaking. "The commander is on his way!"

Sure enough, the door to the *Attlus* began to lower, finally allowing access to the vessel. The commander obviously didn't trust anyone in port.

Paranoia, a bad thing if it controlled all your actions, but good if it saved your life. A lesson her father taught her.

Azteriya quickly hugged her best friend. "Remember,

don't tell my parents what I've done until the ship jumps out of this sector."

"I know."

"And tell them it was the Zonian vessel searching for that missing chit to slow their pursuit." Because Mother wouldn't just let her only child run off. She'd send Father to fetch her.

Dorrys sniffled. "Promise to send me a message as soon as you can."

"I will!" Azteriya actually couldn't wait to send her first message home detailing her adventures. *I will achieve a glorious name for myself. Make my father proud.* Surely, in time, her mother would forgive her.

"Get ready to run." Dorrys pulled something from her pocket, a pink furball with four floppy ears and three giant eyes, all of them open wide and unblinking. Dorrys murmured to it.

A mouth suddenly slit open in the furry face, displaying pointed sharp teeth. With a wiggle, the Ygestas took off, sliding down Dorrys' arm, hitting the floor, and, with a scamper of tiny legs, zeroed in on the lumbering commander heading to his ship.

A second later, Dorrys, holding her skirts hiked high at the side and showing off nicely rounded mauve calves, raced out of hiding, squealing. "My Ygestas! It escaped. Someone help me catch it."

As Dorrys chased Bunbun, her pet, round and round the commander, who spun away from his ship, Azteriya darted to the open hatch, legs pumping, not daring to look back but listening for any signs of alarm.

No one shouted, so she could only hope it meant no one noticed. She slipped inside the *Attlus* and then cursed as she saw the shut door leading from the airlock into the ship proper.

She'd not expected it to be closed. She shoved at it. Put her shoulder to it. The yells outside continued. She glanced around and saw a console. She slapped it, muttering, "Open, damn you."

A light flashed, and a sound bonged, the kind that didn't open the door probably on account the unit didn't recognize her biometric signature.

Surely there was a way past it. She couldn't fail. If Mother found out Azteriya had tried to escape again, she might actually resort to the chains she'd threatened.

Azteriya slapped at the panel again, even if it was probably useless.

To her surprise, it pinged and the door opened. She didn't question her luck, especially since Dorrys' excited tone sounded closer, which probably meant the commander neared too.

She moved deeper into the ship, a big ship for one creature, at least only one that she'd seen. Spying meant she'd noted only the commander disembarked, and the terminal scans showed no other large life forms on board.

The commander sailed the galaxies alone. Surely he would welcome some help. At least, that was one of the arguments she'd prepared.

Since remaining around the entrance would get her caught too quickly, Azteriya jogged down the long hall, relying on her memory to guide her straight. She'd studied the design of the vessel, memorizing the layout and plotting out the best locations for her to stow away.

She eschewed the power lift and chose to pop open a compartment hatch. She clambered down the ladder within, traveling two levels before exiting the slim access tube into the engine area. The moment she popped open the panel, the hum of machinery filled the air.

The ship she'd chosen for her escape was a steady older model. However, it featured a new, revolutionary super-dynamic gravitational drive. Which, in simple terms meant no need for wormholes. The ship created its own slips through space, making galactic travel quicker.

The *Attlus* could skip through galaxies at many times the speed of most vessels, and it would take some time before her father could catch up. Hopefully long enough for her to prove she could be a warrior.

Azteriya tucked herself in a corner, a place tight enough to keep her from getting tossed around during the ship's ascent through the atmosphere. The dense magnetic fields in this section would skew any biological sweeps the ship might make, and this area was out of sight of any visual recording equipment.

In spite of her training in patience—galactic units spent in one position in a barren wasteland waiting for her hunting target with her father, long moments spent in silence, body still, muscles cramped less they disturb their prey—waiting took its toll. Excitement didn't want to sit still. Worry, that as with previous times, she'd get caught kept her tense.

No one came to drag her out of hiding. Not a single alarm sounded.

The engine revved faster, the sound an auditory-numbing roar as the ship prepared for take off. She held her breath as the vibration of the craft let her know they'd lifted from the surface.

The *Attlus* didn't shake as much as the small vessels

her father had taken her on when younger to visit the moons. Mother had halted those trips after Azteriya's first fight to go further.

The *Attlus* obviously had excellent seals and environmental controls because her ears didn't plug with pressure. Her stomach didn't drop out. The only way she knew they popped free of the atmosphere was because the slight trembling of the starship ceased. For a moment, gravity didn't exist and she floated, the weightless feeling never failing to bring a smile to her lips. She could still recall her father leaving the gravity off on their trips that he might teach her how to coil her legs and push off using walls. *"Weightless doesn't mean useless."* All his lessons came with an expression. She memorized them all.

Thump. The gravity module kicked in, and her buttocks hit the floor. Her breath whooshed out.

She'd made it off planet.

But it still wasn't safe yet. They were still too close to Aressotle. Close enough that if her disappearance was noted, an armada might be sent to fetch her. Father had connections.

Azteriya hunkered down in her secluded spot, nestled in her cloak. She shut her eyes and took some rest because, as her father had taught her, *When on a mission, remember to sleep every chance you get.* Fatigue could be a warrior's greatest enemy.

Her eyes shut, and she managed a decent nap before she heard it, the heavy tread of footsteps, boots on the perforated flooring.

A glance at her wrist unit showed the elapsed time. By her calculations, they were almost far enough from her world for the super-dynamic gravitational drive to activate.

So close to freedom, but the steps neared. Came toward her despite all her precautions.

While still out of sight, a voice barked, deep and guttural.

Her embedded translation unit gave the words meaning.

"I know you're there. Show yourself. Now!"

Discovery meant no point in hiding. The moment to explain her intent had arrived. Azteriya stood tall and faced the pale and hairy creature confronting her.

She let out an unwarrior-like screech.

By all the moons of her planet, it was hideous!

TWO

OF ALL THE things Jedrek expected to find on board—a critter that hatched from one of the cargo containers, a ghost, which was more common than people knew—a woman, tall and shapely, her skin a vivid purple, her hair a shocking white and bound back in braids, wearing warrior leathers wasn't on the list.

It didn't help she screamed at the sight of him and brandished a knife.

"Foul creature, I shall dispatch you."

"Don't you point that thing at me, woman!" he snapped. Nothing like having an attractive gal call you foul. He'd bathed recently; however, he might not have shaved in a while.

"It speaks!" Such surprise in the tone.

"Of course, it speaks. Not all of us are brain dead idiots." Jedrek hoped his pointed glare let her know who he referred to.

The knife lowered but remained unsheathed. "I was not aware the commander of this vessel kept a pet."

Did she seriously just say that? "Not a pet, princess. A person."

"Are you a mutant?"

"No. I'm a human, from Earth. And enough of your questions. You'd better start explaining who you are and what you are doing on the *Attlus*." And more importantly, where was her accomplice, because Jedrek was acquainted enough with the Kulin and their culture to know they kept their women secluded. It was one of the few civilizations that still treated them little better than chattel.

So the knowledge discs claimed. They'd obviously never met this woman.

Her chin tilted imperially. "I don't answer to slaves. I will speak only to the commander."

"Not happening, princess. I'm not letting you anywhere near him until you tell me where your accomplice is hiding."

"I am alone."

"Bullshit." The expletive, probably not easily translated, made her brow furrow.

"I believe you are accusing me of lying. Yet, I speak the truth. I am alone. I give you my word as a warrior."

At the claim, Jedrek scoffed. "You're a Kulin lady,"—known for their skills of manipulation behind the scenes—"not a warrior, and even if you were, your word means shit to me. I don't know who you are—"

"I am Azteriya Gaw'dessa, daughter of Zuz'eteran, known through the galaxy as the Punisher."

"Never heard of him, or you, nor do I care. You're going back home."

For a moment, he thought she'd stomp her foot. "You cannot return me. I have a glorious destiny awaiting."

"I'm sure you do. But it won't be on board this ship." He jerked a thumb, gesturing for her to get moving. "March that purple butt out the door, princess. I am not starting a war with your planet because you're having a hissy fit and want to piss off your parents."

"I am not a princess!" she stated, quite indignantly. "I am the—"

"You already told me, and I still don't care. As far as I'm concerned, you're a hassle I don't need."

She crossed her arms over a bosom impressively encased in molded black leather—a bosom with only two breasts. Interesting given most Kulin females sported three. It probably indicated some genetic mixing down the line.

"I am done speaking with you." Spoken with the imperial authority of a queen. "Take me to your commander."

He remained unimpressed. "The commander will tell you the same thing I just did." With a few added choice words. "You're going home."

"If what you claim is the truth, then he can tell me himself."

At her continued stubbornness, Jedrek sighed. "Why must you make this difficult?"

"The only one being difficult is you, barbarian." Her lip curled. "I begin to see now why your kind is considered of lower status. It would seem *humans* have difficulty in recognizing their betters and obeying orders."

He blinked at her, the arrogance in her statement stunning, and from such a beautiful woman. Yet, her attitude didn't detract from her looks. He couldn't help but admire them. How could he ignore the fine lines of her high cheekbones, the bright blueness of her eyes, the toned, yet slender muscle of her arms, the indent of her waist, flaring over narrow hips and her legs, long, lean, and encased in crisscrossing straps lined with sheaths.

A good thing he stared. It meant he saw her foot rising to strike him.

Oh hell no. He caught it and meant to toss her on her ass, except she moved and, somehow, he was the one flying.

Crash. He hit a wall and slid down, narrowly missing burning himself on the hot coils of the magnetic gravity system. "Holy fuck, princess. What is wrong with you?"

"I am perfect. You, on the other hand, have some evolving to do," she shouted.

"I need to evolve?" he sputtered. "You're the one that just tossed me like a fucking ball."

"You attempted to touch me."

"Because you kicked me first."

"You deserved it."

"For what? Trying to evict a stowaway from the ship?"

"I am not a stowaway. More like a surprise guest."

He leaned on his elbows, still splayed on the floor, and snorted. "You just defined intruder."

"Not for long. I am going to meet your commander, and he will gladly offer me a spot on this ship."

"Like fuck he will."

"You'll see." She sprinted away from him.

Jedrek jumped to his feet, but she was out of sight, disobeying and escaping. But to go where? Princess was on a bloody ship in space.

"Are you fucking kidding me? Get back here, goddammit!" His roots emerged in his speech, the words of Earth rising despite the two decades spent in space.

The female didn't reply. But he knew where she was going. To find the commander.

He'd better make it there first. Good thing he knew a few short cuts. But just in case that wasn't enough, Jedrek set off the intruder alert. He didn't want the commander to get caught unaware.

THREE

THE UGLY HUMAN, with hair all over his face, one step above a beast, bellowed somewhere behind Azteriya.

"Get your purple ass back here!" But the same way Azteriya didn't obey the animals of her world, she ignored him.

No one took his kind seriously. Humans were but infants when it came to galactic affairs. A protected species because they'd not yet achieved the kind of sentience and knowledge to truly explore the galaxies. Until that happened, they were considered off-limits.

Yet, of late, she'd been seeing them more and more. Why, several Kulin warriors, including her childhood hero, Tren—greatest assassin ever!—had taken some as brides, their physiology compatible enough to create heirs. However, the females she'd seen were much more attractive, their skin smooth and hairless, unlike their males.

The one she'd just met had a hairy face, and the short sleeves of his shirt showed equally hairy arms. It didn't take much imagination to guess the fur covered a good portion of him. No wonder the females of Earth welcomed a pairing with a bold Kulin mercenary. Their bodies below the neck were hairless and smooth.

Although, to give the human male some credit, at least he wasn't puny-sized. He appeared taller than her by a few fingers, and heavy too. She'd wondered when he'd caught her foot if the trick her father taught would work with someone his size. She'd never managed it on her teacher.

However, with the right momentum, size didn't matter.

The human stopped yelling, and she chanced a glance over her shoulder, expecting to see him bearing down on her, only he'd disappeared.

Was he about to cut her off?

She halted and looked, her gaze darting from side to side, attempting to catch a hint of motion. She strained to hear, but the hum of so many components would hide all but the heaviest of steps.

She swept the room again. Nothing but machines, and too many hiding places.

Let him hide. She was going to meet his commander and convince him that it was in his best interest to keep her on board. Maybe she'd offer to rid him of the vermin on his starship while she was at it.

The map in her head of the vessel, hastily memorized once she hatched her plan, didn't tell her where to find the commander. Would he be in his quarters located midlevel? The common area just down the hall from his room? Checking on his cargo perhaps on the topmost portion of the ship?

Given the *Attlus* was still in Aressotle space, the most likely scenario put the commander in the bridge directing the ship.

She'd start her search there.

The size of the craft, built to accommodate its master of fifteen handspans, meant high ceilings, which, in turn, created echoes. Azteriya's feet, while clad in a malleable hybrid leather synthetic, still slapped the tiled floors, the sound bouncing around.

So much for stealth. Then again, her presence was known. That puling human probably gave warning to his master and then hid behind him.

Never assume, the voice of her father reminded. Humans weren't all benign. The scant details she had about them pegged them as a violent species, easy to provoke. On Earth, according to her Barbarian Civilization studies, the strong often prevailed to the detriment of the weak. Females, while given many rights equal to males, lost all protection and were often victims of violence.

But at least they were allowed to wear trousers. Mother would have kept Azteriya in long skirts if she had her way. Never mind a revolution was happening on her planet with the skirts getting shorter, and some even stepping out in slacks.

Azteriya was not allowed to follow fashion. It was her father who'd brought her back several warrior ensembles meant to accommodate her female figure and still allow proper movement in battle.

After her mother burned the first set, Azteriya hid them better.

Her progress to locate the bridge came to a skidding

halt as a portal slammed shut in front of her. No amount of pounding it, or slapping the touch pad alongside, would open it.

"I'll wager that human is behind this." He thought to trap her. He'd find she wasn't easy to snare.

She backtracked, opting for an alternative route, only to find herself stymied as the routes she wanted to take were blocked by sealed portals. Over and over she found herself blocked, herded away from her destination until she found herself trapped in a section of hallway.

No access panel to escape. The touch screens ignoring her demand to open.

He thinks he has bested me!

She wouldn't give in. The tip of her dagger pried at the edge of the panel for the door. Perhaps she could short the mechanism and force it open.

A voice boomed, a mechanical rendition speaking her language. "You will cease your actions at once."

Forget finding the commander, he'd located her. She whirled, looking for the camera. When she found it, she planted her hands on her hips and faced it squarely.

"I am Azteriya Gaw'dessa, daughter of Zuz'eteran, known through the galaxy as the Punisher."

"Apparently not a very good punisher given your flagrant disobedience."

"Who says I'm disobeying?"

"The daughters of Kulin warriors do not leave Aressotle unattended."

Someone knew a bit about their culture. But she wouldn't stop now. She couldn't. "I am not like most daughters. I have a destiny."

"And that destiny involved stowing away on my ship?"

"Because I wanted to petition the commander of this vessel to take me on as part of his crew."

At least he didn't laugh. "I have no need of more crew members."

"You might wish to revise that. I've met your barbarian."

"The Earthling suits the needs of this ship."

"Humans are slow and ugly creatures. I am a warrior."

"You are female. The Kulin don't let their females fight."

Her lips flattened. "An old tradition that needs to be eradicated."

"You think you are the one to effect change?" The tone was flat and yet the query curious.

"All rebellions starts with one person."

"True, and yet you would drag me into your rebellion. I did not come to your planet to start an altercation."

"Are you admitting you fear defying my mother?" She arched a brow. "Because she is the one who will protest the most. My father is the one who trained me. Why else train me unless he meant for me to use my skills?"

"Then have your father take you on his ship."

"He won't. Mother forbade it." For a moment, her lip jutted, and then she straightened and smoothed her expression. "I am asking for a chance to prove my worth."

"No." Spoken quickly and firmly. "I will contact your world and advise them we've located you."

"You'll regret it if you do." Then, despite the fact it lacked honor, she threatened. "If you try and return me, I will tell my father you forced me."

"What?" the machine voice stuttered the word loudly.

"You heard me. If you return me, I will tell everyone who will listen that you fornicated with me against my will."

"You would lie!"

"I won't go back."

"Then perhaps I will just kill you." The words had no inflection, no feeling, and yet she didn't let a chill of fear cool her blood.

Her chin angled higher. "Kill me and my father will hunt you to the ends of this universe and split your armor open that he might rip your innards from your still warm body and feed them to the carrion that fill the galaxies."

"Are you truly bold enough to threaten me?"

"Merely stating what will happen if you don't see the advantage of keeping me on board."

"You are a very unlikeable female. I can see why you are unmarried."

"I will have you know I am in high demand. Dozens of suitors are lined up, begging I take them as a mate."

"And yet you're fleeing."

"Because my worth should be about more than the children I can create in my womb." Too late she clamped her lips tight as she complained.

"Will they not give you a choice?"

She shook her head. "A Kulin's daughter's only worth is in the alliances she makes through mating and the children she births. I want more than that. I deserve more than that."

There was a pause. "You may remain on board—"

She whooped.

"—but don't think this is a vacation. You will work.

With the human, I might add. He is more important to me than you are, so you will treat him with respect."

"Only if he earns it," she muttered.

"You will obey him as you would obey me," the voice barked.

Since she was still hemming on the obey part with the commander, it was easy to nod.

"Crew quarters are on the mid level. Choose a room. Deposit your things, then report to the storage bay for duty."

"Yes, Commander."

"Fail to follow orders and I won't care who your father is. I'll kill you."

As was only right.

The voice ceased speaking, the doors opened, and she smiled.

I did it. I'm going to see the universe. Victory tasted sweet.

FOUR

THE DAMNED WOMAN was staying on board. A bad idea. So freaking bad, and yet it was a done deal.

Even worse, Jedrek had to work with her.

This should be fun.

From what he'd seen of her so far, Azteriya was a spoiled brat who probably never knew a hard day's work in her life.

To give her credit, though, she obviously wasn't completely soft, not with the toned muscles he'd seen. She kept in shape. She also had a few fighting moves. That flip she performed on him was a good one. However it only worked because she'd surprised Jedrek.

It wouldn't happen again.

No letting her get close. Because the temptation to drag her against his chest and kiss her was ridiculously strong. Obviously, he'd gone too long without a woman. He'd have to rectify that in the next port he hit.

It is a long voyage, though. At least two Earth weeks even with the super engine. A lot could happen in two weeks. Perhaps he'd find her more agreeable, and she would—

He shook his head. That direction of thought wouldn't do him any good. She was on his ship as a crewmember. Nothing more. Getting involved would be a bad idea because, what if she really was more annoying than expected or, worse, clingy after sex? Where would he hide?

He'd keep his hands and fantasies to himself—unless he was in the cleansing unit. Then he'd give himself a hand and fantasize as much as he liked with the evidence being evaporated away.

Whistling, more for distraction than anything else, Jedrek was checking on the cables docking the merchandise when princess arrived, sans cloak, still wearing her ridiculous leather gear and armed to the teeth.

"You don't need all those weapons when on board," he said, indicating the various loaded sheaths. If she got too close to a few of the machines exuding magnetism, she might stick.

"Father says a warrior never goes about unprepared."

"We are on a contained ship in the middle of space, about to jump to another galaxy."

"It matters not. Danger lurks everywhere."

"I'm sure even your father strips down to the bare minimum when at home."

"Not entirely."

"But he does. And so should you."

"This isn't my home."

"Oh, yeah, it is, princess, because of your blackmail with the commander." He gave her a pointed look.

"I did not blackmail," she said with a toss of her head.

"Merely showed the commander the less attractive alternatives if he chose to not keep me on board."

Jedrek snorted. "Which is a fancy way of saying bent him over a barrel without any lube."

"What does that mean?" Her nose wrinkled adorably. He didn't mention that though, given he doubted she'd see it as a compliment. She still wore one too many knives on her person.

"It means you gave him no choice."

"He had choices. He just chose the one that rewarded us both. At least he didn't keep me on out of pity. Where did the commander find you? Pet auction?" She arched a brow and smirked.

"Close." He saw no need to hide his origins. "I was part of a slave shipment abducted from Earth."

"The enslavement of your kind is forbidden."

"Which means it's extremely lucrative. There's a thriving trade for human children."

"I can't see why. Given your attitude and lack of enlightenment, I would have thought you'd make horrible servants."

"Even though we're dumb animals"—and, yes, he said it with a sarcastic tone and a roll of his eyes—"there are many who like to impress their friends by having a human to serve them. There are also some that enjoy our kind as a rare delicacy." Children were especially prized, kind of like veal back on Earth.

He'd managed to surprise her, or so he surmised since her mouth rounded. "They eat you?"

"Eat. Hunt. Fuck." He shrugged. "As you keep reminding me, the universe and its denizens see Earthlings as nothing more than barbarians. As such we have little say in our treatment." At least most humans didn't. Jedrek was one of the lucky ones.

"That is the fate of the less evolved." What she said and yet a crease of her brow showed it did bother her a tiny bit.

Really tiny.

"Less evolved?" He snorted. "That's rich coming from a Kulin. Let me guess, your fighting and pompous attitude are so much better."

"They are because I come from a civilized culture."

"I bow to your greatness, princess." Said with mockery and yet she waved her hand in acceptance.

"About time you recognize it, human."

"My name is Jedrek."

"How cute of your master to name you."

Was this chick for real? "My mother gave me that name when I was born." Jedrek Tom Garcia, as a matter of fact.

"Were you part of a large litter?"

His lips pursed. "We are not animals. We are born the same way you are." He knew enough of the Kulin culture to state that. He'd studied up on them before arriving at their home world for their scheduled cargo pickup.

"I guess that would make sense given some of my people have mated with your kind." Her lip curled. "I cannot believe they chose to taint their line that way."

On Earth he'd dealt with racism for being born of an immigrant family. It turned out space wasn't any better, except it wasn't the color of his skin or poor roots that were his biggest fault but the planet he was born on.

Not everyone is like that. Just because pampered princess lived in a glass house where her shit didn't stink didn't mean everyone thought like she did. There were some who treated him like an equal.

Remembering that, he chose to ignore her attitude and words. He pointed to the cargo. "Check the mooring clamps. We don't want this stuff banging around when we slide between galaxies."

"The task seems rather menial." Her nose scrunched. "Shouldn't I be training instead?"

"For what?" When it came to being annoying, she was already a pro.

"Training for when we encounter pirates that dare attack."

"First they'd have to find us. When not in transit between wormhole slips, we're cloaked."

"Even if you rarely encounter space battles, what of when we land on a planet and pillage the villages?"

"We don't pillage."

"But you do land on planets, correct?"

"Yes, but those places are expecting us."

"They are expecting you to attack?" she asked, looking quite puzzled.

"We. Don't. Attack." He spoke slowly in the hopes she'd grasp the words.

"Then why land at all?"

"Because that's our mission. We buy goods and then deliver them."

"This is a merchant ship!" Exclaimed rather than questioned.

"Yes."

"You lie."

He frowned. "Why would I lie about that?"

"Because it makes no sense. The *Attlus* is heavily

armored. This vessel design has not only extensive defensive mechanisms but also assault ones too."

"And?"

She flung her hands. "And this ship was built to attack things, not deliver items. Where is the adventure in that?"

"There is no adventure, princess. This is how normal beings make a living. They work."

"Fighting is work."

"If you're a mercenary. Which you're not. What you're suggesting is attacking people for the hell of it and stealing from them."

"It's not stealing."

"Is the stuff you're taking yours?" he asked, one eyebrow cocked.

"No. But if the owner is dead, then it belongs to no one." Spoken with a smug smile.

"What of the heirs?"

"What if they're dead too?" She grinned, and he noted the flat edge of her teeth, not sharpened like the males of her world.

"What is wrong with you, woman? You can't just go around killing people and taking their stuff."

"Why not?"

"Because it's not nice. Do you go around murdering your neighbors and stealing from them?"

"Of course not. We don't pillage other Kulin. Unless they've wronged us. Then we apply for a feuding license from the government and the best warrior family prevails."

"And you call my race barbaric," he muttered.

"It's a civilized manner for dealing with disputes."

"It's insane, and I'm pretty sure this discussion with you has killed some of my own intelligence. So I'm done. We've got work to do. The jump is happening in less than an hour." He turned from her—before he gave in to the urge to shake her and then kiss her dark lips until she stopped spouting nonsense—and walked away.

"While you deal with the menial ship tasks, I shall hone my skills for when we encounter some foes."

"There's no foes, princess," he yelled. Avoiding pirates caused less damage.

"We'll see about that," she shouted back. "I shall discuss the merits of a mercenary lifestyle with your commander."

"He won't listen." Jedrek did his best to ignore the woman after that. She was obviously deranged. Still, he couldn't deny she was also fascinating, in a dangerous, she'd probably chop his hand off if he touched her kind of way.

As he checked the moorings, he could hear her, thumping about, uttering short exclamations, the whistles of something being moved rapidly through the air.

Despite his determination to ignore, he couldn't help peeking from time to time—and to his disgust, he stared as well.

Azteriya had chosen to work on her battle stances in a clear area between the crates, moving her body through a fluid set of routines. Lunging, parrying, roundhouse kicks, back flips. The woman was agile, appeared ready to fight, but would she freeze when faced with a real combat situation?

Because while he'd spoken the truth, altercations were mostly avoided, sometimes fighting did happen.

And when it did, being prepared would make a difference.

Once Jedrek checked all the moorings, he headed back to the front of the storage hold, which meant passing by her. She'd paused and leaned against a crate, head tilted back, a flask to her lips.

A light sheen of sweat made her skin glisten. A pulse beat at the front of her throat, not the side like a human. She finished drinking, her lips moist and inviting.

He looked away.

"Do you know how to fight?" she asked suddenly.

"Some," he admitted with wariness.

"I'm surprised. I didn't think slaves were allowed to learn."

"I'm not a slave."

"Obviously, or you wouldn't be so impertinent."

He shot her a glare. "It's not impertinent to stand up for myself. Or do you think I should just let you insult me?"

"It's not an insult if it's true."

"What's true is you're a rude and pampered brat who ran away from home."

The flask was stoppered and tucked away, the motions slow and deliberate. "You don't have the right to judge me, *human.*"

"I can do whatever I like, *princess,*" spoken in the same sneering tone.

"You know nothing of why I left."

"Don't I? You want to escape a society that values women as little more than brood mares. You wanted to see worlds beyond yours. Experience different cultures.

Prove to yourself that your worth is more than the child you can carry in your womb."

With each word, she almost flinched, proving he hit the nail on the head.

"I am more than just a carrier of a male's seed!" she exclaimed. "I won't have my life bound by ancient values."

"So, in other words, you want to be judged for who you are? How ironic that you won't do the same for me."

For a moment, he thought he'd gotten through, that she finally noted her hypocrisy.

But apparently she'd been dropped on her head one too many times. "I see what you're trying to do. Goad me into fighting. If you wish to test my skills, you just had to ask."

Those words were the only warning he got before she came at him, no blades in hand, but she moved quick. The first fist she launched took him in the jaw, snapping his head sideways. She knew how to hit, but he didn't let her land a second blow. He moved, ducking and weaving, blocking the rapid shots she fired at him.

He brought up his arm, and her fist smacked it. An upraised knee protected his balls.

He went into defense mode, keeping his body parts safe, but he didn't hit back.

She eventually noticed. "Are you incapable of attack?"

"I can attack," he muttered, ducking under a round-house kick.

"Then hit me," she demanded.

"I can't."

"Did your master program you with a detonator that

will cause your body to explode into meat chunks if you attack a sentient being?"

"What? No." He stopped for a minute, and she clocked him. Hard.

For a moment, he forgot she was a woman. Rage enveloped him, adrenalizing his body, causing his body to move in automatic. The next thing he knew, he'd managed to topple Azteriya and pinned her to the floor.

He couldn't have said who appeared more surprised.

"You didn't blow up," she exclaimed.

"Of course I didn't. I never said I couldn't fight."

'Then why didn't you hit me?"

Despite knowing it would get him in trouble, he said it. "Because you're a girl."

FIVE

THE INSULT HIT her like a slap.

He didn't hit me because I'm female?

"Apologize!" she growled.

"Nope. Because it's true. I might not have seen my mother in twenty years, but that doesn't mean I forgot what she taught me. Boys don't hit girls."

"I'm not a girl. I'm a warrior." Heaving her body under him, Azteriya tried to dislodge him. However, the human had her truly pinned, the entire weight of his body holding her down. His strength greater than she would have expected.

As for her arms and hands? He held her wrists manacled in his fists. Leaving her...vulnerable.

Fight him. She knew how to hurt a male in this position. Father had taught her, and yet, she didn't maim him.

Didn't slam her head into his face and shatter his nose.

Didn't ram her knee into his soft parts, inhibiting his ability to procreate.

Didn't do anything at all to hurt him because of her surprise.

A surprise at the fact his soft parts weren't that soft.

Something hard pressed against her lower belly. While innocent in the ways of the flesh, she knew what it meant.

The human was attracted to her! More appalling, her body felt an answering warmth, a warmth that coerced her into lying under him, enjoying this rare moment of feminine vulnerability.

"Resistance is futile." His lips quirked as if he laughed at some inner jest.

"You will have to release me eventually, and when you do, I shall destroy you."

"Do that and the commander is liable to eject you out of the nearest airlock. You heard what he said. Play nice with me."

"He said no such thing."

"You're right, he said we had to work together, and I am working really hard on not throttling you. Good thing you're not a man."

"Stop insulting me."

He leaned close, his gaze intent. "It's not an insult for a man to notice the fact you're a woman. Which is why I won't hit you, even if provoked."

"You say you don't advocate violence against my sex, and yet, here we are, with you atop me." She arched a brow.

"Lying atop you doesn't hurt anyone."

No, on the contrary, it felt rather nice, which irritated her. "I don't like it."

"Well, I don't like being attacked just because you've got some deep-seated issues to work out."

"Don't mock me."

"I won't so long as you don't play victim. You started this."

"I was testing your capabilities."

"Then I'd say you got exactly what you were looking for."

But she hadn't been looking for the languorous heat spreading through her limbs. Never expected the desire that would throb between her legs, giving her the urge to wiggle her lower body.

She needed distraction. "Why aren't males supposed to hit your females?" On her world, it was considered dishonorable to beat females. A warrior should only ever fight a worthy opponent. It made her father teaching her all that more rare and special.

"The same reason your planet doesn't let girls go off and fight."

The reminder made her grimace. "Because we have other duties."

"Like making babies and cleaning the house and being a good wife." He smirked. "Sounds like our kind might not be so different after all."

He dared compare them? She thrust at him, heaving her body hard enough that she managed to roll them. He didn't resist, and she found herself straddling him.

This put pressure on a part of her that usually only throbbed when she self pleasured.

And I like it. By all the moons in the galaxy, she enjoyed it, the breathless sensation, the tingling between her legs.

His expression went taut as she shifted, subtly she thought, to test this interesting friction.

"What are you doing?" he said, his tone low and rumbling.

She leaned forward and smiled. "Showing you we are nothing alike. Nothing at all."

"You're right, we're not." It was he who rotated his groin under her, causing a jolt of pleasure.

She bit back a gasp. "What are you doing?"

"The same thing you are. Being a tease."

"I am not a tease." Said with indignation.

"Says the woman riding me. If you want to fuck, just say so. I'm more than happy to accommodate."

She slapped him. A satisfying smack that turned his face only a moment before he returned that intense stare to her. "You really have a problem with the truth, princess."

"I do not wish to fornicate with you."

"You want me." Spoken so smugly.

"What I want is to kill you." Mostly because he was right. She did want to see what would happen if she kept rubbing.

"Then do it." He angled his head back. "Go ahead. Slash my throat. Or crush it. You keep telling me how tough you are. Let's see it."

The dare left her no room to wiggle. Yet she did wiggle—atop his erection.

Why did it feel so good?

He chuckled. "Like I said. You want my body. Why not admit it, princess?"

"Because it's a lie."

"If you say so, princess." The mockery heavy in his words.

Ding. Ding. A bell chimed.

"What is that for?" she asked.

"Time to jump. Find a seat to strap in."

The excuse gave her the strength to finally fling herself off him, her tender bits aching. She didn't look back once as she stalked off.

Want him indeed. She did not have any interest in the human. None at all. She'd prove it. Despite there being seats for jumping beside him, she chose her room for the next part of the journey. Stayed there until she was hungry.

I'm hiding.

Not hiding, just staying clear of the human so she didn't kill him.

You only want to kill him because he spoke the truth. She did feel some odd desire for him.

She ignored it. Just like she ignored him for the next several sleep rotations. She did her best to not see him, or speak to him, but failed miserably at thinking of him.

The recollection of his body pressing plagued her. Her own flesh betrayed her, yearning for something she couldn't define.

Was her mother right when she said one day Azteriya wouldn't be able to deny the needs of her body?

Had she waited too long to become a warrior? Would her desires now get in the way?

They'd better not because she'd not come this far to fail because of her feminine side.

She fought it, and eventually they reached their destination. The commander's robotic voice boomed through the speaker in her room.

"Get ready, crewmember Azteriya. We are going planet side. You will provide security."

"What of your human?" The moment she asked, she banged her forehead on the wall. *Don't show interest.* She'd done so well avoiding him thus far.

"He will remain behind on the ship. Arm yourself and meet me in the airlock. We dock shortly."

Excitement moved her into a jog to her quarters, where she hummed as she wound her many straps around her body and slid knives into them. She did not have any firing weapons. Projectiles were for those that lacked the courage and strength to fight face to face. They also could be quite dangerous on a ship. One little hole could destabilize an entire structure.

Prepared—with enough weapons to take over a small city—Azteriya made her way down to the airlock, and waited.

And waited.

Jedrek happened by and leaned against the doorway. "You're early."

She tried to ignore him. Ignored his tousled hair, the thick fur on his jaw, and the way his body filled out his shirt.

Why am I staring?

She looked away. "The commander said to be prepared."

"We aren't docking for another half-hour."

"I will wait."

"You seem awfully anxious."

"I am not afraid," she retorted.

"Never said you were, more like itching for action. I can understand that. I'll bet you're feeling cooped up on board."

"The ship is rather limited when it comes to space." Her jogging several times a cycle meant she knew every inch of the vessel. The sight of it got boring quickly.

"You know, it's a nice planet we're going to. They've got a few cities that welcome outsiders if you want to stay."

"Your subtlety in trying to oust me has been noted, human." She sneered. "Try to contain your jealousy that your commander has chosen me rather than you to protect him on his mission."

He snorted. "You think I'm jealous? Have at it. I've got better shit to do than meet with some alien dudes and swap merchandise."

"Then why are you here?"

"Can't a guy pop by and wish you luck?"

"I don't need luck."

"Ah yes, because you have mad skills." His tone mocked.

"You will not goad me into fighting today, human. I see what you're doing. You wish to discredit me in front of the commander."

"I doubt the commander would care what you did because he's apparently a moron where you're concerned," he muttered.

"Your jealousy warms my blood."

"How about you don't spill any of that blood on the ground."

She bared her teeth. "Your insult of my skills is noted."

He sighed. "Must you take everything I say as a challenge?"

"Your very existence offends me." Especially the way he invaded her dreams. Naked.

"Whatever, princess." He strode away and left her alone again to contemplate the coming mission.

A mission she knew nothing about. It didn't matter. The commander thought he might have need of protection, and she'd provide it.

The commander's voice, as robotic as ever, emerged from the concealed speakers. "All crewmembers brace yourself for planetary entry."

She sat on the bench and looped her arms through the metal brackets. There wasn't much jostling or shaking, just a pressure in her ears that popped as soon as their trajectory smoothed. The atmosphere must have been denser than Aressotle. She'd make sure to check the breathability of the surface air.

There was a slight shudder as the ship landed, and then the constant vibration of the engines lessened as they were set to idle.

And still she waited.

She checked the landing site specifications. Heavier gravity, so everything would require more effort. Air was a little thinner on oxygen than she was used to, but her body would be fine for a while before weakening.

She read everything twice.

And waited.

Clomp. Clomp. Clomp. She heard the commander coming before she saw him. She stood and held herself at attention, eyes straight ahead.

The moment he entered, the top of his armored head

almost touching the ceiling, she saluted him. "Commander."

His metallic voice boomed in the small space. "Crewmember Azteriya, I see you are overly prepared."

"I am ready to protect my commander."

"There should be nothing to protect from. This is a simple transaction. We're delivering the goods, and they're paying for them. Nothing more."

A merchant mission. She did her best to hide her distaste and not grimace. "Even the most benign of transactions can go awry. Should that happen, I will defend you."

"How about you don't frukx anything up. And, by that, I mean stay quiet and don't do anything stupid. Jedrek has spoken of your headstrong attitude and violent tendencies."

Her lip curled. "The human should keep his opinions to himself."

"That *human*," the machine generated voice managed an inflection, "has been with me longer than you. You might want to be more respectful."

Respect a lesser being? The very idea almost made her laugh. She bit down her disdain.

The door to the outside opened, the hydraulics lowering the door to form a ramp. As the pressure inside and outside evened out, there was a hissing of gases. An orange-hued light, a natural illumination caused by four suns, lit the space and provided a warmth that felt good on the skin after the perpetual chill of space travel.

The commander moved to stand in front of the open doorway, but she darted ahead of him and ensured she exited first.

The first thing she noted was they weren't on any kind of landing pad. On the contrary, they were parked amidst a field of flowing fronds, their red tops waving due to a delicate breeze wafting fragrantly.

"We aren't in a spaceport," she remarked.

"The clients prefer to conduct their business away from prying eyes."

"I'm sure they do," she muttered, already suspicious. Beings who wished to avoid port authorities weren't the type to always have honorable intentions. It made her more alert.

She made it to the bottom of the ramp, arms extended, a dagger in each hand. Her gaze darted from side to side, looking for movement and danger.

Clomp. Whir. Clomp. The commander followed before she'd given him the all clear. She shot him a dark look.

"You should have waited inside while I scouted the area."

"I've been here before. There's nothing to fear."

Fear? She didn't feel any such thing. On the contrary, her body thrummed, alive with adrenaline.

She crept forward, her boots crushing the slender foliage. A whirring sound had her twisting around to see a compartment opening on the ship. A mechanical arm emerged, gripping one of the shipping containers.

It set the large box on the ground with a loud thump.

The noise hid the arrival of their buyers. Only instinct had her whirling to see them, a trio of short beings, wearing red robes that blended with the stalks, their hands tucked in their sleeves, the hoods lowered, revealing bulbous bald heads, orange skin, their single eye pure white. They lacked noses and ears like most bipedal races but had a thin slash for a mouth.

Ugly. Short. And probably not much of a challenge. Pity. Perhaps she'd make them taller when she wrote to Dorrys back home.

A piercing noise emerged from the robed alien in the middle, the mouth opening wide as it wailed its hello. "Greetings, mighty Tyttan, commander of the *Attlus*."

"A fine day to you too, Rattius."

The single eye stared without blinking. "You are late with the shipment."

Clomp. Whir. Clomp. The commander approached to Rattius before replying. "The supplier needed more time to gather your order. You doubled it from last time."

"It is all there?" asked the leader, his head pivoting that his white gaze might peruse the container.

"Every last drop."

The leader waved at his party, who scurried over to peek inside the shipping container.

"All present," one of them shouted.

"Of course it is, and you can avail yourself of it once you give me payment." The commander held out his huge metal hand, the three fingers extended.

The sleeves of the robe parted, and a hand, more like a thick appendage tipped in a claw, emerged holding a sack. "Your payment as agreed."

Rattius tossed the bag, and Azteriya snatched it mid-air, noting that it seemed rather heavy. Exactly what had the commander traded for the cargo?

"What are you doing, crewmember?" asked the commander.

"Checking the payment." While she thought

merchant tasks beneath her, Mother had taught her to always verify transactions.

"What insult is this?" asked the creature in the robe. "Do you cast aspersion on my honor?"

"You had no problem checking out the goods we brought. Just returning the favor and checking yours," she replied, struggling with the knot.

"Take the bag and get on the ship," ordered the commander.

"As soon as I make sure he hasn't fleeced you." But she stopped her struggle with the knot when she noted Rattius raising his arm.

"This insult shall not go unanswered." Then Rattius whistled, a long piercing sound that had no word, but Azteriya knew what it meant.

A fight!

"We are betrayed!" She might have crowed it a little more happily than necessary. She dropped the bag and readied her knives.

The commander rumbled, "What have you done?"

Nothing yet, however, given the frantic movement of the fronds, as if something moved through them in large number, she had a feeling she was about to earn her keep on board.

A wave of red robes poured from between the stalks in the field, mouths open wide on a battle cry, scythes in hand.

"Permission to engage." She bounced on the balls of her feet.

"Granted."

With a cry of joy, she charged the double-dealing merchants. Dancing around the group, she sliced with her knife, having to adjust her stance and battle moves to their shorter stature.

Clang. She blocked the swing of their curved weapons. She slid to her knees and swung her daggers. Never pausing or looking to see if she hit her target. If she missed, she'd know soon enough.

Instinct had her raise a blade to block. *Clang.* She stopped it. Her other hand stabbed behind. A yell let her know she'd hit her foe.

The pungent smell of blood filled her nostrils. Screams, some of attack, others of injury, echoed all around. As did her laughter.

She kept count of those she downed. Her first true battle. Sure, she'd fought with her father back home. She'd gone on hunts and bled creatures before. But those were animals. Not sentient beings with weapons who could fight back!

But the fact that they could think meant she couldn't make a mistake. She moved fast. She had to in order to avoid injury. She rolled and ducked, slicing as she did, sending the enemy toppling.

"Bring the draeygofyre," a voice screamed.

She had a moment to wonder what it meant before a newcomer emerged from the fronds, a large hose in hand, his eye covered by a single lens goggle.

Flames spewed from his nozzle, and she felt the heat of it as she sprinted out of its path, right in front of the cargo container.

Which ignited.

"No! Not the shipment," someone yelled.

She didn't care. She dodged her way toward the creature with the portable torch. When she got close and he aimed her way, she snagged a wiggling body and held it before her as a shield, throwing it away from her when it caught fire.

It hit the wielder of the flame, and they tumbled to the ground. A few slashes of her knife meant they didn't get up again.

Victory.

"Release the vompeer."

The lull in battle meant she heard the command and could stand ready. What would they throw at them next?

The big lump of black fur emerged from the stalks low to the ground. It leapt and threw itself at the commander, who batted it away with a closed fist.

Before the hissing beast could rise and attack again, the commander aimed his arm. The tips of his three blunt fingers shot a white-hot laser blast that ashed the thing.

But it was only the first. More of the furry things emerged, and Azteriya found herself laughing anew as she fought them off. These creatures were a bit tougher to kill than the robed beings. Their flesh less yielding, meaning she had to strike harder.

Her sword bit deep into one lunging with pointed teeth and red eyes. She struggled to wrench it free from the falling corpse.

Another kill.

A glint of metal in the sun's rays caught her attention, and she turned to see a muzzle—a projectile weapon, how unsporting—aimed at her and firing. She ducked but knew she wouldn't be able avoid the spray of pellets entirely. However, she tried, putting her arm over her head and face.

Plink. Plink. Plink.

The metallic bits hit something, and she cautiously peered out to see the commander had thrown himself in front of her, a shield that took most of the damage.

The one wielding the weapon kept firing and screamed as the commander thumped toward him on hydraulic legs. A cry cut short when Tyttan lifted him by the neck and crushed it.

As for the one who started it all? Rattius turned to run. He didn't go far. The hilt of her knife protruded from his back.

The sounds of battle died. Possibly because there was no one left to fight.

Bodies littered the ground, a few twitching, none of them rising. The cargo flamed, not worth anything, not anymore.

As for the bag she'd tried to check? She noted it split open on the ground, spilling the rocks it held. Plain gray pebbles of no worth.

She pointed. "I knew it. He was trying to cheat you!"

The commander ground the evidence with his big booted metal heel and said, "Let's go back to the ship."

Keeping an eye on his back, they left the scene of carnage—her first true battle!—and she made sure to catch an image to send before activating the mechanism to close the ramp.

Only once the airlock shut did the commander slump. He hit the bench inside hard. It was then she noticed it. Red fluid leaking from his armor. Something had managed to penetrate.

"You're injured," she noted.

"A flesh wound."

"We need to get you to the infirmary."

"I need to get us off this planet before we're attacked." The metal voice somehow managed to sound weary. The commander heaved himself to his feet and swayed. "*Attlus*, prepare a course for the dust quadrant. Maximum speed. Cloak us as soon as we leave the surface."

"Yes, sir."

Azteriya's eyes widened as the new voice replied. "Who is that?" She'd thought Jedrek the only other crew.

"My ship."

"I didn't know it spoke." It certainly never talked to her.

"Because you're not the commander."

The ship shuddered as it began its ascent.

The commander put a hand on the hall, as if to steady himself. He took a few steps, exiting the airlock, entering the hall.

Crash.

Darting out of the airlock, she found the commander splayed on the floor. Obviously more injured than he claimed.

I have to get him to the medical bay.

Or she could toss him out of the airlock and take over his ship.

For some reason, the idea didn't sit well. A mercenary didn't turn on his or her allies.

Azteriya grabbed him by the shoulders and tried to heave him, but his weight proved too much. She'd need help.

"Jedrek!" she bellowed. The lazy human didn't respond. She slapped a control panel, opening the communication channel, and bellowed his name again.

Still nothing. Probably off sulking somewhere because he'd missed out on the action.

There had to be a way to get the commander to the medical bay.

His armor. Maybe if she removed it, he would prove light enough to carry. Or she'd kill him and the problem would solve itself.

She began looking for clasps, finally locating one on the breastplate. The suit hissed, and something clicked; the helmet shifted.

Gripping it with two hands, she twisted and pulled. The helmet came off, and she cursed. Cursed so loudly and thoroughly her father would have applauded and her mother run for a priest.

Because the commander was none other than Jedrek.

SIX

THE MOLASSES RUNNING through Jedrek's veins tried to keep his eyelids shut. Consciousness proved slippery to hold on to, but he kept a grip on it mostly because of the cursing.

"Lying human! Hiding behind a suit."

Oops. Princess had discovered his secret, which he'd expected to happen sooner or later. He was surprised it took this long actually. Then again, in her arrogance and insistence that humans were lesser beings, it probably never even occurred to her that he was more than he claimed.

She sucked in a breath and kept going. "No wonder I was never allowed to meet the commander before going planet-side. You knew I'd figure it out."

More like afraid she'd react psychotically. He did his best to ignore her ranting and the cold throbbing in his body. He'd not expected to get shot. Research said that Rattius and his tribe eschewed modern weapons. They actually had a planetary treaty banning them. Apparently, they'd lied. Even worse, Azteriya had been right to suspect them.

Not that he'd admit she was right. She'd never let him live it down. He groaned and fluttered his eyes open.

A vivid blue gaze stared only inches away. "Don't you die yet. I have questions for you."

"Don't you mean a harangue?" he grumbled.

"How dare you not tell me you were the commander."

"Can you blame me given your attitude about humans?" he asked as he sat up and eased his injured body out of the metal suit. It was harder than expected given his hands trembled.

"I can't believe a human was the one giving me orders this entire time."

"Orders you continually ignored."

"Obviously, my subconscious knew better than to obey. The very idea of a Kulin warrior being subservient to a human."

"You're not a Kulin warrior; you're a crewmember of my ship," he growled, not in the mood to deal with her attitude.

"Your ship?" Pitched in a high note. "Humans aren't allowed to own ships according to the Galactic Charters. Anyone caught selling Earthlings and other barbaric cultures advanced technology—"

"Is subject to death. Yeah. I know. Hence why the previous commander had me adopt the suit before he gave me the ship."

"Someone gave this to you?" Incredulity marked her words.

More like inherited once Klardivus, who originally bought a lost human boy at auction, saving him from the dinner pot, retired. "Can we discuss this another time? I've got to make sure the ship isn't under attack." Plus a few holes to fill. His side ached, and his shirt was soaked with blood. However, he was more concerned with the fact that they'd left a pile of bodies behind.

Getting shorted on a deal happened all the time. So did killing those who cheated. That didn't mean that it wouldn't result in retaliation.

He lurched to his feet, and the room swayed. Damn Rattius. His guys probably laced the pellets shot at Jedrek with something.

He blinked away the fuzziness and stumbled his way to the bridge, Azteriya at his heels, still bitching. "You should be in the medical bay."

He held his side, putting pressure on the wound. "I'm shocked you care."

"I don't. However, you are dripping blood all over my starship."

"Your starship?" He cast her a side eye as he sank into his commander seat.

"Yes, mine. You can't own it. Therefore, I claim it."

He snorted. "You ain't claiming shit, princess. The ship is mine." The only thing of worth he had, apart from a growing credit account—a dented one given the upgrades he'd given the spacecraft—and he was damned if some spoiled purple princess was taking it from him.

She planted herself in front of him, a warrior goddess covered in blood and soot, eyes flashing bright blue, and so damned sexy it almost made him forget he was hurt.

"Do you mind? I'm trying to fly the ship."

"I'm not stopping you."

"Says the woman standing in front of me blocking the view. Get out of the way."

"Make me." She cocked her head as she dared him.

He lunged out of his seat, but dizziness sat him back down hard. A shake of his head didn't clear it. "Thizzz izz bullshitz." He slurred, the change in position making him dizzy.

"You've been drugged," she stated, kneeling in front of him.

A denial sat on the tip of his tongue, but the sluggishness in his veins stopped him from speaking the lie. He retained enough wits to know one thing. If he passed out, there would be no one to control his ship. No one to give orders if they were attacked or something happened.

He closed his eyes as he did the unthinkable. "*Attlus*," he spoke slowly, trying to enunciate the words, "should I be incapable of giving orders, then you are to obey crewmember Azteriya."

"Yes, sir."

"Azteriya?" He said her name as a query mostly because he couldn't see her anymore. Darkness filmed over his vision.

"What is it, human?"

"Don't break my ship."

"You mean my ship."

He might have retorted, but a slumbering beast took hold of his consciousness and swallowed it whole.

When he next woke, it was to find himself in a medical unit.

Naked and tethered. He somehow didn't think it was for erotic pleasure.

"Princess!"

SEVEN

HAVING EXPECTED THE BELLOW, Azteriya did her best not to rush.

The human had spent way too much time convalescing. Really, how long did it take to heal a few wounds?

No, really, how long? She'd never seen actual injuries before. Those who got hurt went to the medical centers on her planet. Either they came back fixed or not at all.

In her lifetime, she'd only suffered minor wounds and breaks, nothing that required intensive care. They had healers with the best technology to fix them.

However, on the ship, she was the one who had to initiate the healing unit. Had to wait and watch as the poison was leached from Jedrek's system and his pallor turned from a sallow gray to the more oddly tanned hue he sported.

As she and the ship had learned to work together—with her yelling at it, "Imbecile machine, what part of find me something to kill don't you get?" with its flat reply, "Please specify a destination"—she'd shared her time between the bridge and all its confusing lights and panels and the med bay, where she stared at his still body.

His lying human body.

Commander indeed. It stuck in her craw that she'd not suspected. Then again, she'd never actually met the commander in person. Jedrek claimed the thing inside the armor preferred to keep to himself. She never thought to question it. As for Jedrek, the male never said or did anything to reveal the truth.

What an underhanded thing to do.

Brilliant too.

A human had found a way to circumvent the laws, and no one knew. No one but her.

It put her in a position of power.

Head held high, Azteriya kept that in mind as she entered the medical bay and did her best to appear aloof. After all, she cared nothing for the human. As a matter of fact, she merely kept him alive because of his knowledge of this ship. Father had taught her to fight, not pilot. On her planet, transportation was automated. Get in a vehicle, tell it a destination, and you arrived.

But this ship...it required precise commands. She couldn't just tell it to find a planet she could pillage. She didn't know the stars and galaxies beyond her own. Which meant they drifted in space. Literally. She'd somehow managed to have the ship stop moving, and now it sulked.

Why else did it not obey her when she spoke? For that reason alone she needed Jedrek—and not because an odd discomfort made her internal organs ache at the thought of his death.

Taking a deep breath as if preparing for battle, she entered the room. "Finally, it awakens," she stated, doing her best to hide any joy she felt at seeing him conscious.

"Untie me this instant," he raged from the bed. He strained, his body heaving, his face turning a reddish hue that reminded her of the Toemmatto beasts. Except when they got too dark, they exploded. Should she take cover?

"Calm yourself," she ordered.

"I'll calm myself when you remove the rope from my wrists and ankles."

Ah yes, the tethers. He'd thrashed quite a bit during his illness. Rather than hold him down, she was practical. "They are there to ensure you don't cause yourself injury. The poison took a toll on your fragile human body."

"Did it not occur to you to use the synthesizer to remove it from my blood?"

She peeked at the machine, the one with all the buttons and no instructions. Rather than admit ignorance, she changed the subject. "You seem rather agitated."

"Could it be because you fucking tied me up?" he yelled.

"The correct term is frukx," she said. "Really, if you're going to blend in, then you should learn how to properly speak."

"I am going to throttle your scrawny little neck, princess." The words growled from him, and the threat of violence made her smile.

Much better than him lying there pale and still. "Is that any way to thank me for saving you?"

"I wouldn't need saving if you hadn't caused the fight in the first place."

Caused it for good reason. "Those creatures were trying to cheat you."

"But you didn't know that until after you started a fight and killed them."

"Yes, I did kill them. A rather goodly number too. You're welcome. If I'd not removed so many of them, you probably would have suffered a more fatal outcome." She'd acquitted herself quite well. *I wonder if Dorrys got my message and pictures yet.* Surely, once she showed Mother, her matron would finally grasp that Azteriya was meant to be a warrior.

"You are a lunatic."

"I think your injury has addled your wits. I am perfectly lucid. I think what you meant to say is I'm accomplished."

"No, I meant crazy."

Her gaze narrowed. "For a male currently incapacitated, you should be nicer."

"Fuck nice. I was nice to you when I let you stay on board instead of shipping you back home so your mommy could marry your purple ass off to some poor unsuspecting idiot."

"I wouldn't have married."

"The male population thanks you for that."

Did he imply she'd make a poor mate? "I would make a warrior a delightful mate."

"Considering what I've seen thus far, highly doubtful. You're argumentative, violent, arrogant, and not womanly at all."

The insults pricked, even if they were mostly true. All but the last. "I am extremely feminine."

"You keep telling yourself that, princess."

"You find me attractive."

"You wish. I like my women to be soft. Gentle. Womanly." Spoken with a sneer.

His insistence only served to make her determined. "You are attracted to me," she insisted.

"Nope. I don't like you one bit."

For some reason, the insistence angered her. "I shall prove you a liar." She clambered atop the recovery unit, straddling his body.

"What are you doing?"

"If you think I am so unappealing, then this won't cause a reaction at all." She lowered herself on his groin and squirmed.

"Get off me." Said through gritted teeth.

"Why? It's not like your body cares if I'm atop it, rubbing."

"I don't feel a thing." He glared.

She felt a moment of doubt as nothing hard prodded her bottom. She wouldn't lose this battle. "I'm sure if I were to unlace my bodice and display my breasts, you wouldn't care at all." At times, she wished she had three like her mother and the other females. Alas, she was stunted and only had a pair—like a human—but they were hugely bountiful.

Having read up on Earthlings while Jedrek lay comatose—for information of course, not interest—she knew the males were visual creatures when it came to attraction. The mammalian glands apparently held a particular fascination.

She exposed them, and his breath sucked in. His eyes stared. Her aureoles shriveled as if a cold wind kissed them.

The heat in his gaze made her want to cover up and preen at the same time.

She cocked her head and smiled. Gave a little wiggle. "Still going to claim I'm not attractive?" The erection pressing hard against her sex stated otherwise.

"Fine. You have a banging body. Is that what you wanted to hear? I'd fuck you, but it doesn't mean I like you."

He didn't like her?

Who cared what a human thought?

I do.

She didn't care to examine why. She leaned down, the tips of her breasts brushing against the sheet covering his body.

"You don't like me because you know I am far superior to you."

"No, I don't like you because you're a snob. I prefer nice girls. Easy girls are even better. The kind who don't play games."

"What kind of game do you think I play?"

"You're a cock tease. All talk, no action. I'll bet you've never even kissed a guy."

"Kissed?" She frowned as she sat up. She knew what he meant. Had even seen it during her research. It was the pressing of lips together. She just didn't understand the allure. On her planet, only the sexually deviant strayed from proper fornication techniques.

He laughed. "Yes, kissed. And don't say you have because I can tell from the expression on your face you've never done it."

"Why would I? It seems a useless action."

"Virgin." He stated the word as if it were an insult.

She glared. "Only mated pairs fornicate."

"Because the women on your planet are chattel. You do what the men tell you."

"I do not!" Indignantly spoken. "If I obeyed my parents, I would not be here."

"Please. You went on a teeny, tiny adventure. You killed a few things. But you're too cowardly to do anything else." He taunted.

Challenged.

He accused her of being afraid.

She feared nothing. Especially not the boring press of lips. *I'll show him.*

Leaning low, she touched her mouth to his.

A zap of electricity startled her, and she drew away. "What was that?"

"Attraction, princess."

"I am not attracted to you."

"Then kiss me again."

"I have no need. I've proven my point." Proven that, even tied up, he was dangerous to her.

"Afraid?" His gaze dared her to try again.

She knew she shouldn't. There was something happening to her, happening to her body when she touched him.

She ignored the warning and did it again. Kissed him. At least she thought she was when she pressed her mouth, but he laughed, the rumble trembling against her lips.

"That's not a kiss."

"Our mouths are touching," she mumbled.

"A kiss means you're tasting. Like this."

He showed her, his mouth moving over hers, dragging

across and starting a tingling. He licked the seam of her mouth, drawing a gasp. He took advantage of the parting of her lips to insinuate his tongue.

He put his tongue in her mouth, and she liked it.

No, liked was too weak a word. It set her aflame, ignited a throbbing low in her belly. Set her body to squirming atop him, the friction of his erection against her giving her more pleasure than her fingers ever managed.

The kiss kept going, and she understood what he meant by taste, as his mouth still held the minty freshness of the medical unit that kept him hydrated. The more he chewed on her lower lip and sucked her tongue, the more her body trembled, the harder she ground herself against him.

A fever invaded her body, and she uttered noises as she ground against him. He made noise too, moans and grunts. He even whispered, "That's it, princess, ride me. Ride me hard."

She couldn't stop. Couldn't stop the build of pressure and pleasure. When he said, "Give me your nipple," she didn't stop to wonder why or question. She tore her mouth from his and presented it.

He latched onto the tip, sucked it, tugging hard enough to send a jolt right down to her sex.

It tipped her over an edge. Sent her body rippling into a climax that tore a surprised gasp from her. Her channel clenched and rippled, vibrating her entire body with a bliss that left her limp.

She collapsed atop him, smothering his face with her body until he mumbled, "Can't breathe."

She rose slowly. Her body still tingling with awareness, her breasts feeling heavy. Her lips pleasantly sore while, between her legs, she throbbed.

"How did you like your first kiss?" He sounded so smug.

She clambered off him with a nonchalant, "It was nice." Which might have sounded more authentic if her knees didn't buckle.

His knowing chuckle didn't help, and she felt an odd heat in her cheeks. Had the human infected her with a fever?

Before she could accuse him of having barbarian germs, an alarm sounded.

"What is that warning for?" she asked.

"Proximity alert." He struggled in the bed. "Let me go. We might be under attack."

"I will handle it."

"You don't have the first clue how to fight with my ship."

"I'll learn. I'm good at fighting." Just look how quickly she managed to get a battle going with Jedrek every time they spoke.

"This isn't some game, princess. We're in space. The slightest misstep could kill us."

"Then we will die with honor."

"How about not dying at all?" he yelled. He strained. "Let me go, goddammit. Stop being so bloody stubborn."

Now he sounded like her mother. She didn't listen to her either.

"I will go see what is happening."

"Azteriya! Come back here."

She ignored him. He was probably right. She didn't

know how to truly fly this ship. Thus far, the computer had done all the work.

But how hard could it be? After all, a simple human had learned to do it.

A short while later, when the ship went silent and dark and the cold began to creep because the enemy ship did something that knocked out their power source, she had time to regret not freeing Jedrek.

Especially when something breached the vessel and a gas penetrated even the bulkhead of the bridge.

A gas she couldn't fight with a knife.

An invisible enemy that put her to sleep. Coward. *I am going to...*Zzzzzz.

EIGHT

AWAKE AGAIN. The good news was Jedrek no longer found himself bound to a bed.

And that was the end of the good news.

Things were imminently worse considering he'd gone from blue-balled tied to a bed by a purple vixen intent on killing him with sexual teasing to tossed in a cell, the stone and dirt floor stained and smelly from fluids he'd rather not contemplate.

Pushing himself to his knees, then more slowly to his feet, Jedrek's body protested the abuse. Too bad. He needed to find out what clusterfuck he'd gotten yanked into and how to escape it. Fast. Because cells never boded well.

The first one he'd ever encountered, aboard the alien slaver ship that stole him from summer camp, was a rough transition for a boy used to a soft mattress and three meals a day.

The metal grate of his first prison, meant to allow fluids to pass through for easy sluicing, bit into tender skin. The bowl of thick paste the abductees were granted once a day might have had all the nutrients his body needed but made him gag with each mouthful.

The next cell after the slaver ship didn't prove any better. Dozens of children, crammed in a large room, taunted by the guards with stories of what would happen to them after the auction.

After Klardivus bought him and took him away from that horrifying existence, Jedrek swore to never be a prisoner again.

Yet here he was because of Azteriya, because he had no doubt this was her fault. Stubborn woman. She'd obviously gotten them captured somehow. Mentally cursing her made him wonder about Azteriya. Was she in a cell somewhere too? As a woman, she had even more to worry about than him. Add in the fact a Kulin female was rarely seen off planet without a cadre of warriors and her danger mounted.

Her own fault. She should have let me go to fly the ship.

Much as it irritated him, he grudgingly admired her spirit. He'd seen enough sexism in the galaxies to understand why she fought so hard against the role society wanted to impose on her. Problem was not everyone was nice like him.

"About time you woke up." Speak of the devil. Her voice rang out, and he whirled to see her several cages over to his left looking rather bare without her leather straps and weapons.

Her hair wasn't held back in its usual tidy braid. A bruise marked her cheek, a reddish blot on her mauve complexion. She wore a simple toga, and not a single knife.

I'll bet that made her happy. Probably how she'd gotten the bruise in the first place.

But he refused to show any sympathy, not when her actions had brought them to this.

"This is your fault. Had you released me—"

"You would have flown us away from the pirates who boarded our ship, gassed us to sleep, and brought us to this asteroid."

"Exactly." How surprising for once she recognized what she'd done wrong.

"I am so glad I left you tied up, or we'd be missing out on all this fun." The woman grinned.

Fucking grinned.

"You fucking lunatic." Said slowly so her simple mind would understand. "In case you haven't noticed, we are prisoners."

"I don't know if I'd say that."

"We're locked in a cell."

"For now. And as cells go, they are rather sparse. Good thing we won't be staying in them long."

The urge to ram his head into a wall to hopefully make sense of her words hit Jedrek strongly. "I highly doubt whoever went through the trouble of capturing us is just going to let us go."

She rolled her eyes. "Of course they are not letting us go. We were brought here to fight!"

"How do you know this?" He glared at her, annoyed by many things, including the fact that she wasn't frightened at all. Which meant he couldn't be afraid either.

"The fellow in the cage beside you told me all about this place. Apparently, we're on an asteroid that runs illegal gaming rings."

"Lac'uus?" That was the most famous one run by the crime lord Jakk'ohb A'Diabbloh.

"No. Apparently, that one got destroyed by some Rhomanii prince. This is the new and improved Lac'una."

"What's so improved about it?" he asked, glancing around with distaste at the already rusted bars and stained ground.

"Improved because they finally got a fighter of quality." She struck a pose.

He deliberately ignored it. "Who did they get? Do I know him?"

"Me." She glared.

He snickered. "I think you were misinformed, princess. They don't want you to fight."

"Then why else capture me?"

Did she really not grasp it? "Because you're a female. And given some clients are rough with them, they tend to need a constant fresh supply."

Her eyes widened. "They expect me to fornicate?" Her gaze narrowed as she snarled. "I shall show them the error of their thinking if they try."

"Don't do anything stupid. Which I know will be hard for you. Try and behave. Don't draw notice to yourself while I figure a way out."

A plan she completely and willfully ignored the moment the jailor, a reed-thin fellow at least nine feet tall, slouched in, keys jangling at his side. His canvas trousers, cinched tight with a rope, hung off his three hips. He no longer had his third leg.

She grabbed the bars and yelled through them. "You.

Miscreant with the foul stench. I wish to speak with your employer at once."

"Good, because after what you did, he wants to talk to you too."

"What did you do?" Jedrek asked.

The guard answered. "Killed a few guards and a client who paid handsomely for her services."

"Your employer was impressed with my skill," she said with a sage nod. "Understandable. It is why he wishes to meet me."

"Meet you. Yes. You could say that." The deep guffaw sent a chill down Jedrek's spine.

However, oblivious to the danger, Azteriya exited her cage to follow the guard.

Jedrek gripped the bars. "Whatever you do, don't drink or eat anything they offer. It might be drugged."

"You worry overly much, human." She waved at him.

And then princess was gone.

He didn't want to worry about her. Really he didn't. However, in many ways, she was naive. Her father might have taught Azteriya to fight, but she had no common sense when it came to the dangers of the galaxies. No idea how hard it was for females in a still male-dominated universe.

Hell, Jedrek was a guy, and he constantly had to be on his guard lest someone try and take what was his.

Speaking of his, they'd taken his princess.

My princess?

Well, he had licked her, and she had come for him, even if he had little to do with it. Only because his hands had been bound. But he'd been there when she came, seen the way her eyes closed in ecstasy and her lips parted on a cry of delight.

Now someone else would try and touch her. She'd probably kill them. Then they'd try and kill her. And he was stuck in this stupid cage.

I need to get out of here.

He banged on the bars.

Wham. Wham.

Occupants in other cages lazily rose to their feet to stare.

"Banging he is, why do it he does?" asked one tall and chunky green fellow with pointed ears.

Jedrek explained. "I want to speak to someone in charge."

A shorter red male, in a loincloth that did little to conceal his masculine attributes, pressed his face against the bars. "Aren't you a pretty boy. Maybe they'll have a different fate for you than the arena." The lascivious lick and wink evoked a deep shudder.

"I'd rather fight than fuck on demand."

At that, both the green and red fellows snickered. "We're not in these cages as contenders. We're considered too puny and unworthy."

"Then why are we here?"

"Food. We're the reward to the monsters that win."

"Everyone in here?" Surely the Ymp lied. "What of the female they took?"

"The one who's been making the master's army look bad?" The red creature, who looked just like a miniature devil from Earth, chuckled. "She'll be feeding the master of this place. He likes his food with a bit of fight."

Slam. Jedrek's forehead hit the bars, and he closed his eyes for a moment.

I won't feel guilty. She brought this on herself.

"You might be able to watch the show. The master likes an audience for when he feeds."

At those words, he lifted his head. "How can I watch?"

"Get chosen as the next meal. First come the fights. Then when his pet monster wins, the master gives him a treat, then while his creature is noshing, he then chases down his own dinner."

"So, in order to save her, I have to not be eaten." Not exactly his idea of fun. But what other choice did he have? "All because she wouldn't untie me," he muttered under his breath. Actually, it had all started when he didn't kick her off his ship when she stowed away. Too late to change things now.

He could only go forward and do his best to survive. Survival meant escaping this cage. When the jailor returned, Jedrek was ready—and convinced insanity was contagious—because he banged on the bars hard enough to get chosen.

Here was to hoping he was fast enough to evade the belly of the beast.

NINE

EVENTS WERE NOT UNFOLDING as expected. First off, those running this supposed fighter planet wouldn't give her weapons. They laughed when Azteriya asked for some.

Then, they compounded their transgressions by telling her she was to provide fornication. After she killed a few guards and a male who thought his puny dick would impress, they let her stay a short while in a cell—where she got to see Jedrek—before taking her to some kind of staging area.

"I don't want to wear a dress," she stated, crossing her arms over her bosom.

The red-skinned female, her features wrinkled, her shoulders drooping, shook her finger at her. "You will wear what the master orders."

"Your master can suck it." A human expression Jedrek had used more than once. Much like it stymied her, it also baffled the servant.

Not for long, though. "Grab her. The Kulin female needs to be prepared."

It took six large guards—the seventh and eight off wailing that Azteriya had broken bones—to hold her while servants bathed, perfumed, and oiled her skin until it gleamed. They brushed her hair until it crackled and left it loose. To top off their transgressions, they dressed her in a filmy gown, a sheer white fabric that clung to her breasts, dipped in a vee to her navel, then hung to her ankles with slits up each thigh. It left little to the imagination, and she found it humiliating to be dressed so femininely.

No respect for her warrior status at all.

"If you think this attire will make me fornicate, you are mistaken," she said with a grimace of disgust at the soft silk.

"Your chance to provide pleasure of the flesh has passed. You've been selected for another duty." The deflated red female gestured to the guards. "Take her to the arena."

The arena? Wasn't that where the fights occurred? Finally, she was getting what she wanted.

The wall of bodies around Azteriya was unnecessary. She would have skipped to the arena by herself if someone gave her directions.

Walking into the stadium, she took a deep breath and felt at home. The walls of it were comprised of rough-hewn rock, splotched in some areas with dried ichor and blood. The stony ground didn't fare much better, its stains more plentiful, and some of them fresh. The violence that had occurred in this space spoke to her.

The guards guided her to a dais in the center, where a

creature stood, taller and thicker than her, his skin a deep gray, his tusks pointed and yellow, his three eyes each a different shade.

"Master, we've brought the female as requested." The guard thumped his chest and stepped back, all of them did, leaving Azteriya alone.

The three eyes perused her, and the being leaned in and sniffed loudly.

"You smell delicious," he announced to the delight of the crowd that roared approval.

"Whereas you could use a bath," was her wrinkled-nose reply.

Jagged teeth emerged in a grin. "I intend to bathe in your blood and wear your entrails as a necklace."

"That assumes I am going to stand still and allow you to disembowel me." She shook her head. "And we both know that won't happen."

"You won't be able to stop me. I am the all powerful master of this place. Obey me or face my wrath."

"Wrath of what? Your breath? Any warrior worth his weight knows better than to leave a scent trail that can be tracked."

"Be quiet!" the creature yelled.

"Make me." Because if her family couldn't shut her up, then what made him think he could?

He lunged toward her, and she easily dodged his grip.

"You're slow," she remarked.

"Your resistance is pointless."

"Not so pointless given you couldn't catch me if you tried."

"I don't need to catch you. Guards, hold her still.

Guards?" The male stylizing himself as master peered behind her.

"About your guards. They might be kind of dead."

She heard his voice and whirled. Azteriya found herself inordinately pleased to see Jedrek striding across the stadium floor, a loin cloth hanging low on his hips, looking sexy and dangerous.

Despite her initial shock when she'd first met him, she'd had time to get used to his tanned flesh, the color like a thick creamy syrup on a dessert her mother made. He was still furry, not bare like a Kulin, and yet, it no longer bothered her.

She'd had the chance to stroke it while he recovered and found it to be soft. It made her wonder what it would feel like to rub against.

Naked. Like the videos. Videos that got her thinking about so many things.

There was a roar, and she frowned as she looked upon her delinquent host. "Must you make that noise?"

"You will pay attention to me." The master thumped his chest.

"But you are ugly." She pointed to Jedrek. "He is not."

"He is dinner."

"You are going to eat him? Won't that make you too full for me?"

"Not me! That." The large fellow pointed at a portcullis.

"Those bars are going to eat him?" She learned something new every day.

"No. The—" The gray male shook his head. "Never mind. Release the knovakian beast."

Jedrek paused, his gaze fixed on her before he sighed.

She thought he might have mouthed something along the lines of "Why me?"

Why him indeed.

"I want to fight the monster." She might have pouted as she said it.

"You're my dinner. He's going to get eaten by the knovak."

"But he doesn't want to. Look at him. A puny human. Would you really dishonor your pet monster in such a manner?" she argued. "Much better that a mighty Kulin warrior fight."

The master sneered. "If we had one."

At that rejoinder, she scowled. Sexism wasn't just alive on her planet. Everywhere she went, no one took her seriously. "You are making me angry." And Father told her, *When angry, channel it and destroy anyone who irritates you.*

"Don't worry, princess. You take care of Rhino over there, and I'll handle whatever comes out of the hole."

Had Jedrek just given her a foe? She might have smiled. At least he thought her capable of fighting.

Jedrek pivoted to face the opening, the bars receding to leave a maw of darkness. He rolled his shoulders, impressively wide shoulders actually. He had a decent musculature to him, toned and defined. She could even forgive him the nipples the males of his species so oddly possessed.

What a waste given they only served as ornaments incapable of feeding their young.

From the dark cave something slithered. Something with tentacles that writhed from hiding first, the suckers on the underside of its arms dry and cracked.

She could almost feel pity for it. This beast didn't

belong on an arid world but rather a moist one with oceans.

The knovakian beast lurched out, its body riddled with scars. Of its two eyes, only one stared. The other bore a milky sheen over the surface of the orb.

But despite its injuries and laborious movements, the creature oozed danger, especially given its size alone could crush someone if it fell on them.

As the monster approached, Jedrek stood tall and as unflinching as a Kulin warrior, the comparison startling to her.

He was but a human. A barbarian. Who showed more intelligence than expected. Cunning too. He also had bravery and wasn't a craven coward.

A male who would make strong babes and a good mate.

Blink.

The revelation fled as a tentacle pounded the dirt, right where Jedrek stood. Except he wasn't there anymore. He'd moved and ran toward the creature.

Why closer?

His strategy soon became evident as the tentacles couldn't maneuver as well close to the body. The tips were the most flexible part, but they had difficulty bending to reach Jedrek, who'd tucked against the monster's body.

However, what would Jedrek do next? He had no weapon. Nothing but his hands.

She almost clapped as he dropped to the ground and rose, clutching the broken end of a spear.

He wasted no time, jabbing the beast with it, only it barely penetrated the scaly skin.

He needed something longer. Like the pennant hanging from the stands. But it was too high to simply grasp. She would need a boost.

Azteriya had to time it just right. Ignoring her host's bellowed, "Come back here," she ran at the beast, making sure it noted her coming. Her hair streamed behind her, as did the skirt of her gown, flashing her legs.

The crowd oohed. She couldn't blame them for admiring. They were about to witness great agility and skill. Hopefully someone would tape it and broadcast it.

As Azteriya ran, she watched the tentacles. One of them shot toward her. A push of her legs and she leapt high and grabbed hold of the tentacle, avoiding the suckers. The appendage waved, flinging her back and forth. Once again, she timed her jump, springing away from the tentacle, flipping mid-air. She used the momentum of the fling to reach out and grab the long pole draped with a flag.

It snapped off as she gripped it and dropped with all her weight. She hit the ground, bending her knees to absorb impact. When she stood, she held aloft her new makeshift spear.

The crowd, silent for a moment, burst into loud applause.

She almost took a bow. But Jedrek needed her.

Once again, she ran, fingers tight around the pole, picking up speed, remembering all the times she'd gone hunting with her father. She could almost hear his gruff voice, "Don't miss or you'll be eating grubs tonight." Nasty things when eaten raw without any melted sauce.

Her arm drew back, and as she continued to run, she launched her makeshift spear. It soared, high and true, and the one unblinking eye looked right at it before it exploded at the impact.

The monster bellowed. Their host bellowed. The crowd went wild, and Jedrek turned on her and grimaced, covered from head to toe in goo.

"I was supposed to be saving you."

"The proper words here are, thank you, Azteriya. Once again, you've saved my life."

"I was doing perfectly fine on my own."

"You're just jealous my stick was bigger than yours."

"Not all of us are attention whores."

"What did you call me?" She got close, but not too close because he was covered in monster goo.

"I said you were stupid. You could have been killed."

"But I wasn't." She stepped closer, now recognizing his emotion for something else. Concern.

"You can't always act without thinking."

"Are you sure you want me to think? Because, right now, I want to kiss you, but if I were to think about it, I'd know it was wrong." The admission spilled from her lips.

"I want to kiss you too."

She stared at him. And he stared right back. The moment intense.

Fraught with expectation.

His eyes widened, and he shouted, "Look out behind you!"

Whack.

TEN

THE MASTER of this place showed his cowardly colors when he struck Azteriya from behind. Jedrek caught her in his arms before she could hit the ground.

She breathed, so the blow wasn't fatal, but that didn't quell the rage inside him. He gently lowered her and then rose, his eyes blazing with fury.

The so-called master of this place smirked. "The human is upset. Fear not, you'll join your companion, in my stomach." The crowd laughed.

This was all but a game to them. A game Jedrek was about to play, with his own rules. "You shouldn't have done that." Shouldn't have hurt the woman he'd grudgingly begun to like.

Adrenaline still pulsed through his veins. The broken spear in his hand reminded him he wasn't unarmed. He ran toward his host, who drew a pistol from his robes. A huge one with a muzzle big enough to put a window through him.

"Halt or you die." The master aimed.

Jedrek was beyond caring. "You better not miss." Surrendering now wouldn't keep him alive. It wouldn't save his princess.

The only option was to fight, and he knew how to do that. He might be only human, as everyone liked to remind him, but there was one thing everyone forgot.

Humans had been fighting since the dawn of time. They might not fly to the stars yet. They might not have food replicators. Or cloaking devices. But they could kill.

Especially when left no other choice but live or die.

The other thing this idiot and others forgot was humans also had access to the same biological upgrades as everyone else. That's right. Despite not being born on a so-called civilized world, Jedrek had gotten modifications such as more speed—he dodged the weapon fire, seeing the fat bullets coming at him almost in slow motion—more stamina—he wasn't tired at all—and more strength, enough to slap away the thick arms that moved to block his thrust of the spear. A pathetic attempt.

Jedrek plunged the shard of the weapon deep into the master's chest.

As the gray fellow, his pallor turning a pink, sank to his knees, his breath gasping from the deadly blow, Jedrek leaned close to whisper, "I told you not to miss."

Now, the problem with killing the ruler of an illegal fighting planet was...no one knew what to do next.

The crowd went silent. The various guards in the stands all stared at him. Even the monster had quieted and slunk back to its cave to die.

So Jedrek did what any self-respecting male who'd upset the daily routine did. He hefted the dropped gun, smiled at the crowd, and asked, "Who's next?" Then he fired overhead, a big booming shot right into the ceiling.

Clunk. A chunk of rock fell. Then another piece.

He'd like to take credit for the screaming that suddenly occurred and the sudden wailing sirens. However, after the shower of stone, the ominous cracking sound followed. The eerie whistling of a breach meant Lac'una had just lost its seal to the elements.

Which was their cue to leave.

Jedrek hoisted Azteriya on one shoulder, anchoring her with his left arm, and kept the gun in his right. A beast of a thing with too much recoil, but only a moron would try and escape unarmed.

The good news was no one tried to get in his way. People were desperate to escape, the shouting echoing through the rocky passages. The distant rumble and tremors indicated ships taking off even as the planet continued to shudder, a chain reaction having begun.

And this is why they should ban projectile weapons in space!

The steady *rat-tat-tat* of boots down one hall had him heading into another, unsure of where he was going. Stupid maze. The asteroid had obviously been mined once upon a time, which meant there were halls upon halls crisscrossing, and not a freaking map to be found.

Jedrek ended up back where he started, at the cellblock. He would have turned around to head in another direction, but the red devil yelled, "Set us free!"

He and the pointy-eared green fellow clung to the bars. Not his friends, and yet, in this instance, allies by circumstance. Jedrek hadn't come across the jailor, which meant no keys.

He lifted the gun. "Stand back." The boom as he fired echoed, but metal screamed as the lock shattered. Another deafening shot and both the cells were open.

The green-skinned fellow took off with long strides, not even waiting to see if they followed.

The red devil snorted. "He's going the long way."

"You know how to get us out of here?" Jedrek asked.

The thing nodded. "We need to find a ship. Obviously, or we'll die ignobly, either by asphyxiation or freezing. Let's go, hairball."

"Name is Jedrek," he said as he followed the short figure, trying to ignore the flossing between dimpled cheeks.

"And I am Terrible Eviscerating Destroyer, but my friends call me Ted."

"You're an imp, aren't you?" He'd read about their kind.

"That's Ymp. I'm surprised you've never met one of us before." Ted flashed him a toothy smile. "We are legion."

And possibly the basis for many legends on Earth.

"How did you end up here?" Jedrek probably should have saved his breath considering the cool breeze through the tunnels sucked at the air, yet he couldn't help himself. It was better than wondering how they'd escape alive.

"Stowed aboard the wrong ship." Such disgruntlement. "Then I'd hoped to achieve greatness like the renown Fred."

"Fred?"

"Ferocious Raging Eliminator of the Dense. However, unlike Fred, *you*"—not said with delight—"came along instead. I don't suppose you're a prince in disguise?"

"No."

"Of course not. What a waste of a rescue."

The words made no sense, and Jedrek had no time to question because something impacted the asteroid, sending a great shuddering through it.

"What the hell is that? Are we under attack?" he said, bracing a hand on the wall to combat the shuddering.

"More like the breach has knocked the asteroid off its stable axis into the nearby meteorite stream."

Boom. Something impacted the oversized rock again. Jedrek stumbled and hit the wall with his shoulder. He waited for the bulk of the tremors to subside, except they didn't stop, and the whistling became louder, the rumbling more intense.

"This place is about to blow," remarked Ted. "Good thing we're here."

By here, Ted meant a departure bay, filled with cylinders that acted as elevators to the surface where they parked the ships. If there were any ships left.

People crowded the cylinders trying to get in. Any semblance of civility had evaporated with the mounting danger.

With no lines to speak of, the Ymp chose to shove himself between legs and tentacles, forging his own path. Ted even slipped through a gelatinous blob, emerging on the other side with an exclaimed, "Damn, was that as good for you as it was for me?"

Jedrek didn't have the same advantage as the short fellow, but he did have a gun. He fired it, and eyes, some of them on stalks that just rotated, turned to face him.

"Move!" Jedrek barked.

When they didn't do so fast enough, he took aim and fired on the guard lounging in the crowd. He dropped.

The sea of bodies around the nearest elevator parted and Jedrek, princess still on his shoulder, shoved his way into the tube that already held a few cowering specimens.

He elbowed the panel, shutting the door, and a moment later, they were shooting for the surface. The elevator spat them out onto a concourse with bullet-looking trams. Surface vehicles to shuttle people to and from their ships.

Another blast shook the asteroid, and there were screams. Because screaming always helped. He shifted Azteriya's weight. She'd yet to regain consciousness. Probably a good thing. She'd want to stand and fight. She was stupidly, adorably brave like that.

But you couldn't fight a planet about to implode.

The gun trick boomed, and the silver bullet nearest them cleared. Jedrek commandeered it. The door sealed shut, and a computer asked, "Spacecraft designation."

Um. Good question. He had only one answer, and he prayed it would work. "The *Attlus*." Had those who'd captured them taken his ship too?

The bullet lurched into motion, and he swayed with it as it rocketed out of the concourse.

Once past the building, an opaque window appeared, and he could see outside. See the pockmarked surface of Lac'una. The many ships still gathered on the surface, a giant parking lot—under attack.

Not by other people, though, but meteorites. Hundreds, thousands of chunks, big and small, skirting past in a stream; the edges of them were hitting the asteroid, and more would impact given the asteroid was moving deeper into the storm.

Not good for the planet, not good for the ships either. He winced as he saw a small cruiser get crushed.

"What a stupid spot to build a base." And probably why the original miners had abandoned this post.

But Jedrek didn't care about the poor planning of criminals. Up ahead, he spotted the *Attlus*—with its door closed.

"Shit! *Attlus*, open up." Shouting inside the bullet did no good. He scanned the panel. He needed to open a channel to his ship.

The bullet rocketed closer. "*Attlus*, it's your commander, open up."

Nothing.

And they got closer, not slowing at all.

"For fuck's sake, computer, unless you want to sit there and get crushed like a fucking can, open your goddamned door."

A speaker crackled. "Yes, sir."

At the last possible moment, the ramp opened, the bullet shot inside, and he closed his eyes waiting to crash, only the damned thing abruptly halted, throwing him forward.

He caught himself on his hands, only barely managing to not land on Azteriya.

The door to the bullet opened, and a machine voice said, "Thank you for visiting. Come again soon."

Like fuck.

Jedrek no sooner had exited the bullet than it sealed itself shut. It didn't move until he'd exited the surface hatch with Azteriya and slammed the button, opening the door to the outside again.

It rocketed off, and he watched it on screen as the ramp began to seal again. Watched long enough to see the silver bullet get crushed by a rock.

Fuck.

"Let's get out of here," he muttered.

It took some fancy flying to get out of the stream of debris and ships. He ignored a hail for help, "We've been boarded!" and the soon following message, "The legion thanks you for donating your ship to the cause."

Jedrek exited that section of the galaxy and set a course for somewhere he could relax, get his ship fixed, and concentrate on more important things.

Like punishing Azteriya. Because this was all her fault. And it was time she paid.

ELEVEN

AZTERIYA WOKE, the heaviness of slumber slipping slowly from her body as her eyes fluttered open to note the ceiling of her room on the *Attlus* overhead.

My room?

How had she gotten here? Last she recalled, the cowardly master of Lac'una struck her from behind, felling her. An embarrassing fault because she paid more attention to Jedrek than the enemy at her back.

The shame of it.

But at least the human proved himself not completely useless. He'd rescued her. Even managed to get them back aboard their ship somehow.

Perhaps she'd give him some kind of reward for his loyalty. A reward that would pleasure them both. Kind of like the dream she'd just woken from. A dream where naked bodies pressed and mouths explored with wild abandon.

Even the mere thought was enough to make her throb. And she knew just the male to fix it.

She went to rise, only to find herself unable to move.
What's this?

A tug of her wrists showed them bound. A yank of her legs showed her ankles tethered as well.

All the warm thoughts she had toward him fled. A mighty roar left her lips. "Human!"

He didn't reply in person. He chose to use the communication system.

"You bellowed, princess?"

"Release me at once." She glared at the ceiling.

"Here's something that should sound familiar. No. See, I still remember a certain pampered princess refusing to let me go when our situations were reversed."

She remembered too. The hot kiss they'd shared. The rubbing. The pleasure.

"You cannot keep me a prisoner," she snapped.

"Then be nice."

"What?" she sputtered.

"You heard me. Instead of calling me human, why not try using my real name? Jedrek." He then said it more slowly. "J-e-d-r-e-k. Very easy."

"I will tear your entrails from your body and wear them as a belt."

"It's that kind of attitude that's the problem, princess. Why can't you treat me with respect?"

Because he was human. The words didn't emerge, mostly because his query struck a chord inside. Hadn't she herself asked for the same thing with her mother?

Respect me for what I can do, not what I am.

He mistook her silence and continued to speak. "When are you going to admit we're not that different?"

They were plenty different, but...in, some ways, alike. For one, they were both very stubborn.

"I am a Kulin warrior."

"Don't care."

"Humans aren't allowed to own ships or people."

"The thing about laws is they only pertain to the folks that recognize them. As an Earthling, I'm not part of your galactic bullshit. So I don't have to obey them. As a matter of fact, I can do whatever I like, including not talking to you until you decide to be nicer."

"You will release me at once!" She yanked on her tethers, straining and pulling. He didn't reply, and a strange feeling assailed her.

Panic.

She was not used to feeling helpless. Not even in the cage had she felt confined. With her limbs free, she knew she could fight.

But now...now she was a prisoner to his whims.

Like he once had been a prisoner to hers. And what had she done?

Given in to her desires.

Would he do the same?

I mustn't give in. Mustn't allow herself to be weak. She had to resist his flesh. His alien allure.

Yet, his very alien nature was what drew her. His tanned skin fascinated. The hair on his chest and face wanted to be stroked. As for his body? She knew it could bring her great pleasure.

However, a lifetime of teachings made her hold her tongue. She would not apologize for being herself. She would not beg for mercy.

She stared at the ceiling.

The boring ceiling.

Long moments went by. An eternity.

A—

"Let me go!" she yelled.

This time, he replied in person. "That wasn't long. You lasted a whole fifteen minutes."

She had no idea what his time reference meant. Probably several galactic cycles.

"You can starve me and hold me prisoner. I will never give in."

"Is it really that hard for you to say, Jedrek, you're a decent sort?"

"Why do you care what I think?"

The question made him frown. "I don't know. I mean, I shouldn't give a shit, and yet, I lugged your ungrateful purple butt off that asteroid. I could have left you there."

"Why didn't you?"

He neared the bed and shrugged. "Because I'm nicer than you, obviously."

"That wouldn't be hard. I'm not nice."

"You are sometimes." He ran a finger down the sheet covering her body, and it was then she noticed she was nude under it.

"You stripped me."

"The asshole in that arena clocked you pretty hard. You had some brain bleeding going on. So you spent a few days in the med unit getting patched up."

"I almost died." The knowledge she'd almost expired, and so ignobly, widened her eyes.

"Yeah, you did. A funny thing happened while you were in the medical bay recovering."

"What?" The query was spoken softly.

"I missed you." He snorted. "I know that sounds crazy, especially since you're always driving me nuts. Twisting my words. Challenging me at every turn. And yet, there it is. I missed you, princess, and I'm glad you're not dead."

"I am glad too." Perhaps her happiness at not dying was why warmth moved sluggishly through her veins, surely not his statement.

"But here's the thing..." The fingers, still lightly stroking through the sheet, stopped, and she gasped as he pinched a nipple poking. "I don't want to miss you. I shouldn't give a damn about a woman who's done nothing but denigrate me. I shouldn't want you." The pinch turned into a roll of her nipple between his fingers, and a soft moan escaped her.

"The needs of the flesh don't need to be rooted in affection." A lesson taught to Kulin females as their mothers prepared them for an eventual joining with a warrior family.

"But that's just it, princess." His fingers stilled. "I like you, even though I don't want to."

His admission mirrored her own thoughts. Her own inner turmoil. "What shall we do to combat this impasse?"

"Well, apparently, I can't just outright kill you. Or ditch you, so I'm thinking there's only one thing left to do."

Her lips parted.

"Slake my passion."

He said it so boldly.

It was enough to make her realize what he meant. She shook her head. "I will not be raped." Never mind she was tied. She would find a way to fight him.

His turn to shake. "I won't rape you, princess. As a matter of fact, I won't fuck you, even if you beg. I'm horny, not stupid. I know what would happen if I took your virginity."

"What makes you think I am pure of body?"

He snorted. "I know. And I am not about to change that. I don't think either of us want that kind of commitment."

He didn't want to be her mate. Which was fine. She didn't want him as her mate either. What then did he propose?

"If you don't plan to fornicate with me, then how will you assuage your passion?"

"Our passion," he corrected. "There are ways, princess. I'm about to teach them to you."

The very thought made her shiver.

"What if I said no?"

He gave her a look. "Do you want me to walk away?"

The correct answer was on the tip of her tongue, and yet she said, "No."

He smiled. A slow and sexy smile that did things to her. Made her heart stutter.

Then it stopped when he said, "I'm going to make you come so hard."

TWELVE

A SHARP TUG pulled the sheet off her body, and her skin reacted, especially her nipples, which hardened into dark points.

He let himself just stare at her. Not something he'd indulged in while she recovered. There was something wrong about ogling an unconscious woman, but now that she was awake and licking her lips, her eyes at half-mast, he looked his fill at her long and lean athletic body. Nothing soft about Azteriya, except for her bountiful breasts.

"Do not stare."

"I'll do whatever I like, princess. I'm in charge." To show her how helpless she was, he tweaked her bare nipple, twisted it enough that she cried out and arched.

She was so responsive to his touch. Ripe for passion.

And he was oh so ready too. His cock throbbed.

He stripped off his shirt, feeling her watching him. She didn't even pretend to look away.

She bit her lip when his hands went to his pants. Her

gaze widened as he pushed them down over his hips and kicked them away.

"What is that?" She stared at him, her brow creased.

"What?" He looked down. "It's a cock. I know your men have one."

"Under them. You have an exterior sac."

She referenced his balls, and he laughed. "I do. Want to touch?"

A startled gaze met his. "Why would I touch them?"

"Because it feels good. Because it makes me hard even to think of your hand fondling them or taking them in your mouth."

"In my mouth?" She squeaked the last word.

"I'm going to teach you so many things, princess." And, hopefully, finally rid himself of this insane desire for her.

He moved to the foot of the bed. Her thighs were already parted because of the tethers. He stared at her. Stared at the petals of her sex, more pronounced than a human's. But without the clitoris at the top of her sex. Like the males of her species, whose balls were tucked out of sight, the clit was inside. If a cock were to penetrate, it would rub against it.

But he wouldn't be fucking her. Not if he wanted to stay a single man—and a living one.

A finger could reach it, though. Perhaps even his tongue.

He positioned himself on the bed between her legs. She trembled. Not in fear—excitement.

He could see the desire humming through her veins and shining in her gaze.

He let her watch him as he stroked the length of his

cock, the tip of it blushing and full. He used that tip to rub against her moist lips, drawing a gasp from her.

"I thought you weren't going to penetrate," she said.

"I'm not. This is called teasing." A teasing that affected them both as he kept rubbing his swollen head across the wet folds of her sex.

Yes, wet, because she was excited; the honey on her nether lips proved it.

He wanted a taste.

Leaning closer, he ran his tongue over her nether lips.

Azteriya groaned and even hissed, "Yes, more," as he stroked her with his tongue, flicking it across her moist petals, quick strokes that had her hips thrusting against his face.

Her enjoyment made him throb, and it occurred to him there was a way to indulge them both at once. It took but a moment to reposition, his knees cradling her head, his face overtop her sex.

"What are you doing?" She sounded curious.

"On Earth, we call this a 69. Which means you're going to lick me while I lick you." A simple explanation that drew an, "Oh" from her.

She'd soon see, and learn.

He lowered his body until his cock pressed against her lips. Her clamped lips.

"Open up, princess."

"But—"

He stifled further questions by pushing the tip of his shaft into that opening.

Only belatedly did it occur to him that she could bite and cause damage.

To forestall that, he dipped his head and gave her a lick. The soft sigh blew warmly over his cock.

"That's it, princess. Blow me." He huffed a hot breath on her sex. "Lick me." A long, wet one across her trembling lips. "And suck me." He tugged at her, savoring her unique musky taste.

After that, she needed no instruction. Slowly, hesitantly, she tasted him, drawing him into her mouth and then sucking at him instinctively. She quickly understood the power she had over him as the strong pulls of her mouth and lips drew groans from him.

It felt so fucking good, and he planned to return the favor. He lowered his head once again between her thighs and ran his tongue over her delicate lips. He lapped at her over and over, taking great pleasure when her hips began to undulate in time to his strokes.

Back and forth, he swiped his tongue, delving between her folds for a deeper taste of her. He knew he'd found her clit, a round knob just inside, when she gasped around her mouthful of cock. He stabbed at her pleasure button, rewarded by mewling cries that vibrated his shaft and elicited even more of her honeyed nectar.

He couldn't resist propping himself on one arm and sliding a finger into her tight, heated sheath.

"What are you doing?" she asked, pausing for a moment, her body going still.

"Making you come."

He finger fucked her, sliding it in and out, not far, just enough to stimulate her clit, until she came with a scream that he stifled with his cock.

Then it was his turn to yell and his body to go rigid as she sucked him, sucked him so hard he spilled in her mouth. And she took it. Swallowed his cream, and then said, "Can we do it again?"

Hell yeah. The only problem was keeping his promise to not fuck.

Because, in that moment, and the others where they did things—dirty, sexual things that left them sweaty and limp, he wanted to sink balls deep inside her. Mark her womb with his seed and call her his forever.

Problem was, if he did that, she'd probably kill him.

What a way to go.

THIRTEEN

AZTERIYA WAS ALONE, only because Jedrek had left her bed to go check on the status of the ship. She also was untied.

The male had a point when he claimed there was nowhere for her to go. As to taking over the ship, her last attempt had left much to be desired.

For the moment, she let him command.

He did it so well. Especially in bed. She rolled onto her naked stomach and held in a moan. Her skin, overly sensitized, urged her to rub.

Even the slightest brush of fabric made her shudder. Yet, she'd climaxed only moments before.

It didn't seem to matter how many times Jedrek made her body sing. How many times she clenched and cried out her pleasure. She ached for him. Yearned for more, wanted to—

She knew what she wanted. She just couldn't do it.

Instead, she accessed the most recent batch of mail the ship had grabbed as it passed a waystation—places dotted throughout the universes that served as refueling points and message centers. Without telling Jedrek, she retrieved the electronic messages kept in a secret account.

The first one was from Dorrys.

I am jealous of your adventures. You seem as if you're having a wonderful time. I'm not. Mother thinks I should apply to become a handmaiden for the priestess.

Azteriya frowned. Dorrys was too young for such a position. Usually, only widows and spinsters applied because one of the requirements was chasteness.

I don't want to do it, of course. I want to be married. But Mother is refusing to give me a dowry, and now that word is getting around about my handmaiden application, the warriors that are here won't even look me in the eye. I don't know what to do.

The situation wasn't a good one for Dorrys. She could either disobey her mother and find herself cast from her home and living in the wilds or she'd have to escape like Azteriya had. Except Dorrys would never run away.

The next message was dated sometime later, also from her friend.

The application was submitted. Guess I'll be taking the veil soon. I've got to do some purification rituals first. I kind of wish now that I'd allowed Men'ran to propose. He might not have been the best warrior, but at least then I would have my own hearth and a chance at a family. But enough of my woes. I haven't seen any new images. How is your adventure?

Turning out to be a lot different than expected. Sure, Azteriya had found battle, but this thing evolving between her and Jedrek? She didn't know what to do or think about it. She'd left home to escape a mating, and yet now, all she could think of was taking the final step with him.

Your parents are livid you left. But they're hiding it. Your mother is acting as if you're some kind of pioneer, heading out to the stars to find a male because the warriors you've met so far are beneath you.

Trust her mother to find a spin on the situation.

The next message came under Dorrys' name, but it wasn't from her friend.

Don't make me fetch you. Return home at once.

She didn't need a signature to know it was from her mother.

Since Dorrys' account was compromised, she debated sending a reply. What would she say?

How about the truth?

Having too much fun. Met a male. Thinking of keeping him. Miss you.

Because she did miss her family and her home. Her mother, for all her succinct opinions on a proper Kulin daughter's place, was quite simply her mother. A person who'd shared everything in her life up until now. As for her father, how she wished she could share her adventures and let him know his teachings were being put to good use.

In the end she settled for sending, *Not ready to come home yet. Miss you.*

"Why the big sigh?" Jedrek asked, entering without knocking.

"My family figured out I was messaging Dorrys. They want me to come home."

"Maybe it's time."

She rolled onto her back and glared at him. "If you wish to rid yourself of me, say so."

He reached out and grabbed her, pulling her to him.

"Never said that, princess. But you can't avoid facing your parents forever."

No, but for the moment, she could ignore them. She sought his mouth for a kiss. A kiss that led to touching. Pleasure. Climaxing and even more frustration than before.

It wasn't enough. But to ask for more...

Would being his mate really be so bad?

He held her cradled against his body, and she opened her mouth to speak, only to bite back the words as a chime went off.

He pulled away from her and began to dress.

"We're here."

"Where?" He'd not told her of their destination, each time silencing her with kisses and, "It's a surprise."

"The planet of my former commander. My foster home, I guess you would call it."

"You brought me to your world? Why?" Was this his way of saying he also tired of their situation? That he wanted more as well?

"My best friend and foster brother is getting married."

The real reason caused a pang of disappointment. "You go to witness his nuptials. What of me?"

"You're my plus one."

FOURTEEN

WHAT POSSESSED him to bring her here?

Why didn't I drop her off somewhere and put a call in to her parents? He should have ditched her delectable purple ass, but couldn't. His need for her only got worse the longer they spent together.

So he kept her with him. Brought her to his home, a home he'd initially fought when Klardivus first brought him. But the stern warrior hadn't allowed Jedrek's frequent runaway attempts to sway him from mentoring and molding a boy who'd lost his family and his entire world.

In time, his past life faded. Eventually, he understood he couldn't return to Earth, not with everything he'd seen, everything he knew. Eventually, he made himself a new home, a new family.

And part of that family was expanding. His foster brother and best friend, Zayn, was getting hitched.

Azteriya strode alongside him, regal appearing and fierce despite the dress she wore. Her warrior regalia hadn't survived their previous adventure, which meant he'd had to put in an order for clothes when he docked, which were delivered with curious looks, but no questions. Those would come later.

The attire was very feminine and more practical than Azteriya realized. She railed at the short swirling skirt that left her legs bare. The soft-soled sandals that could grip any surface without slipping. The tight-fitted bodice with its winding material.

What she didn't notice was the slits to place the knives, the fabric sheaths within the skirt.

Maezotomia was a planet of fighters, but socially advanced enough that the females not only trained and fought alongside the males but also embraced their sexuality.

Is that why I brought her? To show her that not all cultures are like that of the Kulin? Why did he care? Her viewpoint didn't matter to him.

He didn't give a damn about her. She'd made it clear what she thought of him. Shown her disdain for all things human.

Yet, that disparagement was never evident when they kissed and touched. When alone, there were no barriers keeping them apart. Nothing to halt the passion that always ignited between them. Perhaps removing the social barriers would stifle that flame.

Or allow it to fully bloom and not be something they only resorted to when fighting.

Upon disembarking from the ship, the first thing he saw was his friend. Zayn stood a few paces from the gangplank, as serious as ever, his dark hair hitting his wide shoulders, his countenance unsmiling. A true born Maez, he had the gray/green skin that was slightly scaly to the touch. The golden yellow eyes that could slit and see even in the dark. The build of a football player, wide and beefy. All normal things on this planet.

What was strange was the softening of Zayn's expression as someone moved around him, a shorter being with pale skin and short blonde hair.

A human!

Jedrek's mouth dropped open, especially when his foster brother said, "It is about time you arrived. We celebrate my nuptials this very night. Meet my intended, Clarabelle," he said, gesturing to the woman. "Touch her and die."

Which, to the uninitiated in the Maezotomian culture, was a normal greeting when presenting a mate. The Maez did not share. By declaring this upfront, it ensured no other male would attempt to steal their bride. To even flirt was considered a travesty worthy of going to war.

There were many wars happening at any given time. A good thing the Maez were prolific.

"A pleasure to meet your heart mate, brother. Might I ask how you found her?" Because she certainly wasn't present the last time he visited.

The petite woman smiled. "I kind of crashed here. And then, he wouldn't let me leave." Which apparently didn't bother her one bit given the soft look she aimed at Zayn.

I hope I don't look at Azteriya the same way. If he did, she'd probably blind him.

"And who is this you bring, brother?" Zayn aimed his

gaze at Azteriya, and Jedrek bit his tongue because he almost blurted, *Mine.*

As if. He wasn't about to claim the pompous warrior princess. He could just imagine the shit that would cause, starting with her. She'd never accept a human, as she so sneeringly put it, as her mate.

Stepping forward, chin held high, she took care of her own introduction. "I am Azteriya Gaw'dessa, daughter of Zuz'eteran, a mighty warrior known through the galaxy as the Punisher."

Zayn uttered a whistle. "You have stolen quite the prize, brother."

"He did not steal me." Princess tilted her chin proudly. "I commandeered his ship."

As Zayn's eyes widened—mostly in mirth—Jedrek reclaimed his manhood and exclaimed, "Like fuck you did. The *Attlus* is mine. You stowed aboard. She's a runaway," he explained to his brother.

"It is not running away if I am heading toward a greater destiny."

"What destiny? Killing things is called survival."

"Unless you're paid for it, then it's called business," boomed Klardivus. His foster father arrived, slower due to his advanced years, his skin a deep gray of age, the wrinkles more pronounced.

"Finally someone who understands." Azteriya bestowed a smile on Jedrek's foster father.

The grin was returned. "A Kulin maiden. How rare. How did you manage to lure her and convince her to be your mate, boyo?"

"I didn't. She's part of my crew at the moment." A true statement, so why did she shoot daggers at him?

His father's eyes widened. "And her family didn't kill you?"

"Her family doesn't know." Not entirely true. By now they had to have noticed her disappearance and narrowed down the possibilities.

"It sounds like a fine tale. You'll have to regale us with your adventure while we make the final preparations for the ceremony."

By preparation, Klardivus meant the males and females separated, the one side getting drunk while the other giggled and weaved flowers through hair.

Azteriya actually sent him a look of panic when Clarabelle linked arms with her and went off with her in tow.

He almost went after her. Who knew what kind of trouble she'd cause if left alone?

However, when the brief statement of, "Maybe I should check on her," was met with snapping sounds and a whistle—*I am not whipped!*—he decided against seeking Azteriya out. He'd have to hope no one got killed.

Luck was on his side—or somehow Azteriya behaved for once. The evening passed without a hitch—or a death.

When the three moons rose that night, at their apex, Zayn and his heart mate exchanged vows in front of the entire family and their friends, which numbered in the hundreds.

There was no presiding priest, just the right combination of the moons, the three of them converging into a single line, similar to an eclipse on Earth. The triple alignment bathed the land in a pure silver light, illuminating the couple making the pledge and binding it with the power of the moon.

The words Zayn and Clarabelle spoke rose loud and clear, hanging in the air as if given form and weight.

"From this night, our purpose is one. Our home is together. Our lives intertwined. I pledge to you my devotion and faithfulness. Should any try to come between us, may their blood stain our daggers and their heart fill our bellies for we are now and forever one."

As the words were spoken in tandem, Jedrek couldn't help but look at Azteriya. She stood at the front of the witnesses, her gown a pale blue that contrasted with her skin, her hair unbound and woven with a crown of flowers. Her gaze locked onto his.

As the moon's glow bathed them, he couldn't help but mouth the words of the ritual, mouth them and wish that things were different. That Azteriya stood in front of him, hands clasped, joining herself to him.

Making her forever mine. Foolish fantasy.

Probably the effect of the potent kijar wine he'd imbibed.

Yet, he couldn't shake it, the feeling that he should find a way to make what they had more permanent and binding.

Doubtful she'd allow it.

The ceremony concluded with much cheering. The finding of a heart mate was always cause for celebration —and food.

So much food and wine.

The alcohol flowed like a river into his goblet. Yet, he barely drank it. He didn't thirst. Nor did he hunger. At least not for food.

What he wanted wasn't on the menu. She wasn't even a possibility.

Despite all they'd shared, Azteriya would never belong to him. Which meant his princess was available for other men to pursue.

She was an exotic flower amongst the gray-skinned tribe, her purple skin a colorful contrast, her white hair like a moonbeam given form.

The male warriors, who'd yet to find their heart mates, flocked to her. Flattered her. They showed her their daggers. They praised her when she tossed them at the targets and landed them in the smallest ring.

Her cheeks flushed, and her lips parted to smile. He could almost read her mind. *Finally, people who accept me.* She didn't have to justify wanting to be a warrior among the Maez. She could have the life she always dreamed of.

He should have been happy for her. Happy she found acceptance among the people who'd adopted him.

But...Jedrek was more selfish than he realized. The attention shown her bothered him. It shouldn't have, but it did. The more she danced, her lithe body moving with a sinuous grace reminiscent of the battlefield, the more he burned, aflame with desire and jealousy all in one.

He wanted to stride into the clearing, ringed with trees and lit by moon globes, and shove aside those who ogled her. Stab those who touched. He wanted to drag her into his arms and claim her in the eyes of all that they might understand she was his.

Mine.

He might not understand the need, but it was there. Pulsing, pushing, demanding that he do more than sit, watch, and drink.

But what if she rejected him? She'd made it clear he was good for dallying only. That his genes made him unsuitable.

That didn't stop him from wanting.

What would it take for us to be together?

Nothing from him. He was ready for that final step. It all hinged on Azteriya. She had to make the choice.

FIFTEEN

HE'S WATCHING ME.

Azteriya could feel his burning gaze on her, stroking her limbs, shooting daggers at her partners.

She saw his desire and encouraged it. Noted his jealousy and it made her bolder.

Why doesn't he come claim me?

She could see he wanted to. Yet, he held back.

Could it be because you've told him enough times he's not good enough for you?

It made her remember her mother's words. *You're being too picky.* Of course her mother meant in respect to the Kulin warriors she brought around, but didn't it also apply here?

What exactly did Azteriya want in a male?

Strength. Jedrek had plenty.

Wealth. The male owned a ship.

Courage. He lacked for none.

Respect. Hadn't he shown that when he took her on that first mission?

Attraction. No denying she wanted him.

So what stopped her from taking that final step, from making him her mate?

The question rolled around in her mind. And the answer, when it came, was astonishing.

He hasn't said he wants me.

Sure, he'd pleasured her body. Brought her on an adventure. Even brought her to his home world, but he'd yet to say anything, anything at all, to make her think he wanted more.

Why didn't she just take what she wanted? This wasn't Aressotle. According to the Maez females she'd conversed with before the mating ceremony, it wasn't just the males who got to decide. A female didn't have to wait for a warrior to claim her; she could claim him first. *If she has the courage.*

Does fear hold me back?

What would her mother say if she mated with a human? What would her father do?

Who cared? *This journey was about discovering what I want. About putting my needs first.*

And she needed Jedrek.

Leaving her partner mid-step, she strode to Jedrek, long strides that brought Azteriya to the pile of cushions he lounged on, cup in hand. She loomed over him, blocking the moonlight.

"Something wrong, princess?" His eyes glittered brightly.

"Why do you not dance?"

"Two left feet."

A frown creased her brow. She didn't understand the reference. "Why do you not dance with me?"

"You don't seem to lack partners."

That sounded like definite jealousy, so why did he not act?

Perhaps, he couldn't act. "Do you claim any of the females here?" If yes, she'd have to take care of that problem.

"Why would any of them want a barbarian human male?" He threw her words back at her mockingly.

"Father says a great warrior knows when to admit they might have been wrong."

"Exactly what are you saying, princess?"

She didn't want to say it. Didn't want to speak aloud the fact that she burned for him. Wanted him.

So, instead, she leaned down and grabbed his hand. She always forgot how heavy he was, so it was a good thing he heaved himself upward. His slightly great height meant he stared her almost in the eyes.

Could he read the message in them?

"What do you want from me?" he whispered.

Everything he had to give.

She pulled him by the hand and dragged him into the woods. They left the sound of revelry behind, the flickering light of the torches. Everything faded except for the pounding of her heart and the whisper of expectation.

When she found a bower of fragrant grass and leaves, she pulled him to her.

"Claim me."

"Excuse me?" He blinked at her, confusion on his face.

"I said claim me. As a male claims a female."

"Have you been drinking?" He eyed her suspiciously.

"I am not incapacitated, if that is your query. What

am I to you?" Such a pathetic thing to ask, and yet she had to know.

"You're a crewmember on my ship."

"Is that all?"

"What else should I say? You've made it clear that we can't ever be anything more. That I'm not good enough for you."

She heaved in a breath before admitting, "What if I said I was wrong? That I wanted something more?"

"Don't fuck with me, princess."

"But that's precisely it. I want to fuck you." She intentionally used the Earth term. The crudity of it shocking and yet the most apt way of saying what she wanted.

"Since when?"

"Since I realized that you were right. I want you."

He dragged her close. "Say it again. Say it so I know you mean it."

The words spilled from her. "I want to lie with you. To feel you inside my body." She met his gaze. "I need you. Do you need me too?"

The question caused something in him to snap. He growled, the sound primal and exciting. He mashed his lips against hers, a fierce kiss to go with the raging passion that always seemed to explode between them.

His hands pulled at her clothing, shedding them, while she yanked at his. They formed a blanket for when her back hit the ground.

Their embrace went on forever and yet ended too soon at the same time. The fire of their desire burned bright, and she gasped as Jedrek slid down her body, kissing his way through the valley of her breasts, giving each nipple a hard tug of his mouth, then lower still to her mound. He rubbed his bristly jaw against the tender flesh, and she bucked, knowing what would come next.

She spread her thighs and bent her knees, giving him full access to her body. And he took advantage, dipping his head that he might lick her sex.

It never failed to excite. The hot slash of his tongue. The heat of his breath.

Under his sensual torture, she bucked and moaned. Dug her nails into his scalp, tugging at his hair, urging him to do more.

He slid a finger in her and rubbed at her pleasure spot.

She moaned. It seemed unfair she only got to enjoy it. She scissored her legs around his body and flipped him onto his back. Then pounced.

She reverse-straddled him and, without any warning or foreplay, took his hard shaft into her mouth. He yelled, and his hips thrust up. She took him deeper.

His hands grabbed her thighs and pulled her mound down to his face, and he began licking her again, lapping and stabbing her with his tongue.

She matched his rhythm, bobbing her head, bringing him to the brink of pleasure. He did the same to her, stroking her with tongue and his fingers. Her hums of delight vibrated around his shaft.

She couldn't help but rotate her hips, her body falling into a rhythm that wanted more. Jedrek matched the pace, thrusting into her mouth.

And then she was on her back again. He'd flipped them, and he was positioned between her legs, his expression fierce.

He pressed the tip of his shaft against her sex, but he

didn't push in. His gaze instead sought hers, silently asking permission. She replied by locking her legs around his shanks and drawing him into her.

When he hit the barrier all females were born with, a thick membrane set deep within that would change everything, she drew him down to her, pulled him near enough to kiss.

Then bit his lip.

He roared as his hips thrust, his shaft tearing through, claiming her body as his.

She sucked his bleeding lip as he rode into her, her own hips moving in time, the pleasure building. Intense. So intense.

Hot and powerful. His thickness stretched her.

Oh how he stretched her and filled her, each stroke rubbing against her inner pleasure spot, making her tremble until she could hold back no more.

The intensity of the orgasm left her limp and whimpering, but happy, so happy.

He whispered her name, "Azteriya!" as he thrust one final time into her. The heat of his climax bathed her womb.

They lay close together, their breathing ragged, their bodies cooling. He held her close to him when he rolled as if unable to bear parting.

And she hugged him back.

They spent that night in their fragrant bower. Not fighting. Not worrying about what the moment meant. Just being together. Accepted for who they were.

It wasn't the harsh brilliance of the dawning light from the red sun that woke her but rather the voice that boomed over her. "I've found her. Lock in on our position and teleport."

Father had found her. And there was no chance for goodbyes.

SIXTEEN

HAVING WOKEN BEFORE AZTERIYA, Jedrek let her sleep undisturbed. After the night they'd spent, she deserved it.

A smile hovered over his lips. It had been beyond stupendous.

Mind blowing. Epic. It was a wonder they retained enough wits to dress themselves at one point before sleeping some more because it occurred to Jedrek that anyone going for a walk might see his princess naked. His newly discovered jealous nature had an issue with that.

He didn't worry about leaving her alone in the woods. This section of land might seem untamed, but it was, in actuality, a park. Hundred of hectares of wild growing trees and plants, with the most dangerous thing in them the insects that liked to nibble soft flesh. But those mostly came out at night.

As for two-legged menaces? This was a sacred grove, used for ceremony and the coming of age of the Maez.

There wasn't a Maez alive who would commit an act of violence within it.

Outside of it, that was another thing. Past the boundary of the sacred forest, civilization reigned. Hover crafts zoomed by under canopied trees, the thick boughs forming bridges across. Inside the hollow boles, homes and businesses.

A modern world hidden inside a jungle. It amazed a boy when he first arrived and, as an adult, it still gave Jedrek a thrill to see how the Maez artfully blended modern convenience with nature.

The sidewalk outside the park held little foot traffic this time of morning, most people still abed having celebrated late.

But he knew of one place that was always open, the Maez equivalent of a coffee and pastry shop.

Entering, Jedrek used his palm print—linked to a credit account—to purchase some replenishing fluids—a chocolate-flavored hot brew that was a cross between cocoa and coffee—plus some savory pastries. Flaky on the outside, inside steamy and spicy meat bathed in a salty cream.

Treasures in hand, he headed back to the park, making his way through the familiar paths, only to hear the buzz of voices.

He broke into a jog, not truly worried. No one would hurt Azteriya—*if they do, they die*. While he didn't worry about violence, she was beautiful, and he'd not officially claimed her. He'd have to rectify that on the next triple moon.

Jedrek emerged into the clearing they'd chosen the night before to find his foster father, and another of his brothers, Huudo, standing shoulder to shoulder, while two security personnel ran devices over the ground. They skimmed the equipment over his bed from last night. The empty bed.

"Where's Azteriya?" He didn't spot her anywhere. Perhaps she'd gone to relieve herself out of sight. But why the welcoming committee?

"Is that who was here last?" His father shot him a look from under a creased brow.

"We both were here. We spent the night." Making glorious love, claiming each other under the moons.

"She's gone."

"I see that. Where did she go?" Jedrek couldn't help the terseness of his query.

At that, Klardivus shrugged. "No idea. We got a ping on the security monitors of an unauthorized teleport and came to investigate."

The meaning of the words penetrated. "Someone infiltrated the planet and stole her!"

"I don't know as I'd say stole. I don't see any signs of struggle, and by the looks of your girl, she could have done some damage."

Indeed, Azteriya would have never gone quietly. Unless someone subdued her. Perhaps she'd never had a chance. It could be someone had teleported to the surface, drugged her, and stolen his princess.

"We have to find her. Have you located the vessel that initiated the transport?" It couldn't have gone far. He'd not been gone that long.

"They are working on it." Klardivus pointed to the security team, a female he'd never met, dark head bent to her task, the other a slim fellow tapping on a tablet, relaying her softly murmured findings.

"I'll ready my ship." Jedrek was ready to leave this instant to rescue Azteriya. He didn't know who had the gall to raid the Maez home planet, but he knew it wouldn't go unanswered.

I'll rescue you, princess. Even if he'd wager by the time he reached her, she'd managed to cause a mutiny and take over the vessel. She was glorious that way. Look at how she'd taken over his heart and life.

"Sir, we found the offending craft, heading rapidly towards the Xevion wormhole." A shortcut between galaxies that would lead the vessel to a nexus point with a half-dozen more.

Jedrek would have to reach them before they slipped away and he couldn't track them.

His father slapped him on the back. "Let's get to the *Attlus*, boyo. We'll get your woman back."

"Sir, hold on, incoming message from the transgressing ship."

"Play it aloud," said Klardivus.

"Attention, planet Maezotomia. This is Zuz'eteran Gaw'dessa, known through the galaxy as the Punisher, first rank warrior of the planet Aressotle. Your unlawful detainment of my daughter has ended. At this time, we won't declare war, but should you engage in pursuit, or otherwise detain us in any fashion, your transgression will meet with the immediate cease of trade between our worlds and the commencement of hostile action."

In simple terms, if Jedrek went after Azteriya, it would mean war.

But his foster father didn't care. "Does he dare

threaten us? Bah." The rapier gaze he'd come to know and respect fixed Jedrek. "Say the word, boyo, and we'll go fetch your woman."

And start a conflict? One that would pit two warrior planets against each other? Over a woman?

Not just any woman. My princess.

Even he wasn't so selfish.

He shook his head. "Let her go."

If she truly wanted him, she would have fought to stay.

And if I truly wanted her, shouldn't I fight to get her back?

He went looking for the answer at the bottom of a glass of grog. Dozens of them.

SEVENTEEN

A PART of Azteriya hoped there would be a reply to her father's brazen announcement. Some kind of rebuttal— by Jedrek, his grumbling voice declaring, "Hand her over or we will go to war!"

She was disappointed, for the only message her father received was one simply stating, "We have no wish at this time to engage the Kulin in a war over a female no one has claimed."

And there it was. Jedrek hadn't claimed her. He had no idea she'd claimed him.

No one knew, not her mother or father. They'd just arrived and taken her.

Now she had to deal with the aftermath.

Mother, her arms crossed over her ample three breasts, had finished her harangue detailing the ways Azteriya was ungrateful, headstrong, and determined to bring shame on their house. The next part was about her future. "Since you've satisfied your need for adventure, it is time to return home and do your duty to your people."

"It wasn't a need, mother," Azteriya muttered. "It is what I want. I want to feel as if I'm doing something meaningful with my life."

"Mating the right male and producing heirs will give you that meaning."

"No, it gave your life meaning. I am more than just a womb. I am a warrior." She glared at her mother.

"Why, because you can fight?" Without warning, her mother dove on Azteriya, wrestled her to the ground, and quickly too, and then lay atop her, one arm over her throat. "I can fight too. But that doesn't make me a warrior. Nor does it mean I can change the laws."

"Laws can be changed if enough of us demand."

"Except, those who wish to be like you, to eschew their fate are few, too few to execute a change. And why should your dissatisfaction punish them?"

"Because I'm not happy." Azteriya shouted the words and felt remorse as her mother actually flinched.

Clambering to her feet, Mother smoothed her skirts and expression. "I see. I did not realize I was such a horrid parent."

Azteriya tried to apologize. "I didn't mean it that way."

"Perhaps not, and yet it's clear I've failed you. Failed this family." With those words, her mother sailed out of the bridge, leaving her with Father.

Silence reigned for a moment until she said, "Do it. Lecture me."

"Lecture you about what, following your own destiny? I wouldn't do that to you. But I will give you a piece of advice. Happiness doesn't come from fighting." The statement had her turning to look at her father, who fiddled with the controls of his ship.

"It doesn't come from making babies either," she retorted.

"I wouldn't say that. Making babies is a pleasant thing for both involved."

"Father!"

A grin caught her by surprise. "There is no shame in the act. Just like there is no shame in admitting the greatest joy I have in my life is my family. Which includes you, my daughter. When I first beheld you, and then cradled you in my arms, I experienced an awe and delight never found at the tip of my sword."

"That's easy for you to say. No one's asking you, though, to stay home to care for that baby. You could leave anytime you wanted."

"Yes, I can leave, and I miss you and your mother every time I do. The life of a warrior seems glamorous to you now. The adventure and adrenaline. But that's only because you've not experienced the other side of it, the slogging through jungles on a wet planet, where everything wants to drain you dry of your blood, and your only reward is surviving because the employer was killed and there is no payment."

"I know not everything ends in victory."

"It can also end in companions being lost. Missing out on important moments in your daughter's life."

The frank admission caught her by surprise. "I didn't think you cared about those things."

His lips took on a wry tilt. "Because a warrior is taught from the cradle to not care. To never show or admit it."

"But you're telling me."

"Because you still see battle as a glorious affair. It's not. There are times I wish to retire and never see the inside of a latrine unit in need of repair or shake out my boots so I don't get bitten by a skorpia."

"Then why don't you? We don't need the credits."

"But then I'd be with *her*"—a look shot at the doorway Mother had left through—"every single moment of the day."

"She's your mate."

"She is, and best taken in small doses." He smiled. "We would kill each other if we spent too much time together. By going on adventures, we both have a chance to miss each other and indulge in those moments we have."

Azteriya could understand what he said. She and Jedrek were like that. Sparring and butting heads then doing more intimate things.

No more. He was gone now.

"How did you find me?" she asked. She already knew Mother had hacked the message account she'd set up with Dorrys. They probably used that insecure thread to follow her.

"It wasn't that difficult since I knew where you were. Or did you really think no one would notice you'd jumped on that ship?"

Her eyes rounded. "You knew? And let me go?"

Again, his lips quirked. "It was plain to anyone with eyes you wouldn't be satisfied until you got the adventure you craved. So I might have enabled your escape."

"But Mother—"

"Never knew. She'd have eviscerated me otherwise." Father shuddered, and she giggled.

"Why?"

"Why did I let my daughter with the fiercest of hearts

and bold spirit of adventure go out and fulfill her heart's desire?" He arched a brow.

"If that was your intent, why fetch me so quickly? I wasn't done." What she didn't admit was her uncertainty she'd ever tire of it. She'd discovered a whole other way of living. How could she go back?

"Your mother is tenacious. Once she found out you were gone, she went on a rampage to locate you. I could only delay so much."

Azteriya sighed. "I wish you'd waited longer."

"I take it you didn't find what you were looking for."

Oh, she'd found it. Problem was, she couldn't have it.

More like I can't have him. That, more than anything, was what depressed her.

EIGHTEEN

DEPRESSION SAT on him and made everything a chore. In an effort to fight it, Jedrek got drunk. A lot. Over and over.

It didn't make him feel any better, especially when Zayn arrived, fresh from his honeymoon—known as the Official Creation of an Heir period—and yelled louder than the tapping hammers in his brain could handle.

He winced. "What the fuck, brother?"

"I want to know why you are wallowing."

"I am not wallowing. I am partaking of the fine wines the local vendors have to offer and increasing their profit margin."

"You're getting drunk."

"So what? What's it to you? And why are you here? Shouldn't you be off screwing your new bride?" One of them should be having fun.

"My bride is well pleasured. Probably carrying my heir as we speak, which is why I have time to deal with you."

"I don't need to be dealt with." What Jedrek needed was more wine because his goblet was empty.

"You are being pathetic."

"Gee, thanks. Want to slap me while you're tossing around insults?"

Slap.

Jedrek glared at his brother. "I didn't mean to actually slap me."

"You need it. You need to wake up, brother. Why do you sulk here and wallow in defeat rather than fetching your mate back?"

"She's not my mate."

"Did you not deflower her in the garden of our forefathers under the triple light of the moon?"

"Yes."

"Then you claimed her."

Perhaps in the ways of the Maez, but he doubted Azteriya would see it the same way because, if she did think they belonged together, she wouldn't have fucking left!

Jedrek shrugged. "It doesn't matter what I want. She's gone back to her people."

"The same people she left because they could not provide what she needed."

"And, apparently, I wasn't what she needed either or she wouldn't have gone." The bitter truth spilled out.

"Perhaps she had no choice. A child's duty is to obey their father."

"Without a message to me?" Something, anything that said, *Sorry, babe, daddy's being a jerk. Miss you. Love you.*

"So the onus is entirely on her?" Zayn arched a brow. "I did not realize relationships were so one-sided."

"They're not."

"That means you told her that you wished to keep her and bore affection for her."

"No." Not exactly. They'd said some things but never had a chance to hash out what it meant.

"If you did not tell her, then how was she supposed to know?"

His bleary eyes glared at his brother. "What the fuck is it with all this relationship advice? This doesn't sound like you. What the fuck?" Because, in the past, Zayn had an attitude of screw it but run like the wind come morning.

"Blame my human mate. She made me see that sometimes stubbornness can get in the way of true affection. We almost did not become mated because I refused to admit my need for her. Thankfully, I came to my senses, killed everyone in my way, and claimed her."

"Well, I can't exactly kill those who took Azteriya considering it's her family." Her father's proclamation had made it clear what would happen if Jedrek made a move.

"Have you learned nothing, brother? If you cannot kill, then you injure them instead."

"What are you suggesting? That I just go to Aressotle and kidnap her?"

"Now he understands. Did you know that their history annals speak of an ancient tradition where the warriors stole their brides?"

He snorted. "Azteriya would disembowel a man who tried."

"The question is, would she disembowel you or be glad of your attempt?"

"I'd have to go through her father to find out."

"The man is a warrior, used to injury. So long as you don't kill him or maim him for battle, he will admire your tenacity and skill if you make it past him."

"He's not the only one I'd have to make it past. We're talking about infiltrating a planet full of purple warriors."

"So you bring a team with you. Someone to aid and abet your path to the surface and escape with your prize."

"Are you volunteering to possibly start a war?"

Zayn's eyes widened with a false innocence. "Who, me?" He smiled. "They make a splendid foe, and it's been awhile since we've indulged in a planetary skirmish. Our arenas could use some new blood."

Because the Maez didn't believe in full-scale wars that decimated planets or cities. The cost of destruction wasn't worth it. Instead, they resorted to a more civilized method. Champions and tourneys, where the final fighter standing won the war and took the agreed-upon concessions.

"What if she doesn't want me?"

At the complaint, Zayn cuffed him. "You're welcome."

Jedrek glared. "Just because I taught you the expression 'smack some sense' doesn't mean you get to act on it."

A wide smile said otherwise, which was how Jedrek found himself aboard a ship, not his, it would be recognized, but another that would act as a Trojan horse, an ancient Earth fable that he still remembered decades later.

I am coming for you, princess, whether you like it or not.

NINETEEN

"WE HAVE a suitor arriving for the evening meal period," mother announced.

"Don't you mean victim?" was her father's gruff murmur.

Azteriya almost laughed, except there was nothing funny about her mother's determination to marry her off.

Apparently, now that Azteriya had gotten her small adventure—an adventure sorely missed—she should now be ready to settle down with a warrior and spit out babies.

Well, the joke was on Mother because she wouldn't marry any of those males. "You might want to cancel that meeting," she told her mother. "Cancel all of them because I highly doubt any of them will want to mate with me."

"They are willing to overlook your less than conventional attitude."

"Will they overlook the fact I'm not a virgin?"

At the words, her father took on a grim expression

while her mother looked utterly appalled. "You lay with a male?"

"Not just any male, Jedrek." And she'd not been able to stop thinking about him. Missing him.

"Who is this warrior? I don't think I know the name."

"Because he's not a warrior. He's a ship captain from Earth."

"A human?" Mother's lip curled. "Filthy barbarian. How dare he lay hands on you."

"He dared because I wanted it." Azteriya wasn't about to let her mother malign Jedrek.

"Even worse!" her mother yelled. "You should have killed him for the temerity."

"Fear not. I shall rectify the matter." Father eased out his sword and began sharpening it. "I'll have the ship readied for immediate departure."

The discussion about killing Jedrek made Azteriya snap. "You will not ready the ship. You will do nothing, do you hear me? I will not have you harm the father of my child."

The silence was thick enough to cut.

"You're pregnant?" Mother asked, her expression as flat as her query. "Are you sure?"

"I am. And before you say another word, I am keeping the babe, and no one is killing Jedrek. As a matter of fact, I am thinking of fetching him that we might raise our child together." So many revolutionary words in one sentence. It would have felled most mothers.

Not Azteriya's. Mother's back straightened, and her eyes took on an icy glint.

Azteriya braced for the harangue.

"You will marry him."

"You can't...wait, what?" She fumbled as her mother's words sank in.

"You will marry him."

"But he's human."

"And? So are the mate's of Tren and Jaro. Or are you going to tell me they're not worthy of respect because of their choice in mate?"

"Of course not." They were this generation's greatest warriors.

"I think your choice is just what this family needs," Mother said. "New blood will make your progeny strong. I've heard Tren's child wails loud enough to shake mountains."

"So you approve?" She was so confused.

"I don't," Father grumbled. "Miscreant laid hands on my daughter."

"Because I made him," Azteriya retorted. "Do you really think it would have happened otherwise?"

"Still want to kill him."

"You'll have to go through me first. But fear not, you shall still possibly get to fight. We must go fetch him from the Maez planet. They might not allow us to take him." Jedrek himself might balk. They'd never truly discussed a future.

"Start a war?" Father's expression brightened. "They do have fabulous facilities for battle."

Mother groaned. "Would it kill you to stay home for a short while instead of haring off to another fight?"

"Yes," Azteriya and her father answered together. Mother and Father got along best for short periods of time.

"When do we leave?" Azteriya asked.

"When the dawn crests. I'll have the ship prepared."

Which meant one more period of sleep before she went after the male she should have never left.

Would he be happy to see her return?

These thoughts and more plagued her as she stumbled into sleep. Her mind churned with thoughts of him, his kisses, his groans, the thumps of bodies hitting the floor. The yelled, "Don't make me kill you. Princess wouldn't like it," waking her.

Her eyes were barely open when her feet hit the floor and she fled her room. She emerged into the common area of their home to see her father facing off against an intruder. A shape familiar in size and...

"Jedrek?" The faint light of the moon orb on the wall illuminated his features. "What are you doing here?"

"Kidnapping you."

Father snarled. "Don't you dare touch my daughter."

Before Father could attack, Azteriya tripped him from behind and stepped over him, placing herself in front of Jedrek. She cocked her head. "Why do you want to kidnap me?"

"Because you're my woman."

For a moment, indignation filled her then warmth. A body-heating molten warmth as she realized he'd come for her. "Are you claiming me?"

"Fucking right I am. I should have come after you the moment you left."

He cared. Enough he'd risked death infiltrating her planet to find her. She flung herself at him, and he only staggered a little as he caught her.

"Is that a yes?"

She nodded. "You may abduct me."

"I wasn't asking permission."

"I know." Which, for some reason, caused heat to lick between her legs.

"Just so you know, I follow the culture of the Maez. Which means, since I'm claiming you, any other who touches you dies."

"Very romantic," she sighed. A human word she finally understood. "And I should add that, in the spirit of adopting your culture, any woman who so much as ogles you will lose her eyes."

He chuckled. "Violent, but, then again, that is the reason I love you too."

"You love me?"

"He'd better, invading our home in the middle of the dark period, attacking your father." Mother appeared in her nightdress, brandishing a knife.

Jedrek shot her a wary glance. "Um, princess, I might need my hands."

"Mother won't hurt you."

"Are you sure of that?" Mother's expression gave nothing away. "What kind of dowry are you offering?"

"None, Mother. He is abducting me."

Mother sniffed. "Sycophant, trying to curry favor with me by following our traditions. Where will you live?"

"I don't have a permanent home yet. So probably on the ship for now."

"A ship is no place to raise a child," Mother argued.

"We'll worry about that when it happens."

Azteriya leaned close and whispered in his ear. "It already has."

Thump. Jedrek hit the floor.

Consternation had her frowning at him while Mother

snickered, "Just like your father. We had to get married quick too."

Eyes wide, Azteriya gaped at her mother, who angled her chin. "Don't look at me like that, daughter. Your father was the finest warrior around. I made sure no other could claim him."

"But you told me he abducted you."

"He did, after I refused to marry him." Mother's smile held a softness to it she'd never seen. "He knocked out my father and two brothers to get to me. Still has the scar of the knife I stabbed him with."

To quote Jedrek, mind blown.

TWENTY

JEDREK AWOKE IN A BED. Not alone, nor was he tied.

Azteriya leaned over him, her white-blonde hair unbound and framing her face.

She smiled at him. "About time you woke."

"Maybe next time you think of dropping a bomb, you could give a man warning. Is it true? Are you really pregnant?"

At her nod, he placed a hand on her flat stomach. A belly with his child inside. Holy shit. "I love you, Azteriya."

"I would say your grand affection for me was obvious. I am obviously a treasure without parallel. The future mother of your progeny. A—"

He interrupted. "I love you despite the fact you're arrogant. I loved you before I knew you carried my kid. I love you because you're arrogant and awesome and because living without you sucks."

Her expression softened, and she leaned forward to

whisper against his lips. "I missed you too. I am glad you came for me. I was about to come fetch you."

"You were what?" His eyes widened.

"I decided I required you as part of my daily existence and was set to fetch you after the sleeping period was complete."

"You could have just called and said I miss you, come see me." He would have dropped everything for her.

"But abducting you is much more pleasurable."

"You mean would have been."

"No, I abducted you." Her lips curved into a grin. "In the interest of keeping you alive, Mother drugged you that I might smuggle you back aboard your ship."

"I didn't need help. In case you hadn't noticed, I made it to your place fine."

"Only because my father allowed it. He wanted to test your intentions."

"I take it I passed since I'm still alive?"

"You did. I would never allow anyone to kill you."

Emasculating, but coming from his princess, it said a lot. "So what happens now?"

"Now we go forth and forge a future. You're my mate. You were the moment we lay together and I marked you."

His lip tingled as if in response to her words. The bite. "I'll still need to claim you at the next triple moon in sight of everyone."

"If you must, but in the meantime, I have a need." She shifted enough to yank the blanket covering him free. She straddled him, naked. They were both naked.

His cock noticed and nudged. Her mouth curved into a pleased smile. "Now that is the welcome I was antic-ipating."

"I'll show you a welcome." He gripped her hips and pushed up against her, drawing a gasp.

He watched her, saw her eyes close, her nipples harden, and her sweet cunt, oh so fucking wet. She slicked him with her honey. He couldn't wait to bury his cock. But first he wanted to play. He let his fingers dance over her skin, feeling the heat of her against his flesh, loving how this powerful woman trembled at his touch.

He let his hands roam, teasing her flesh while his hips ground against her, a torture for them both. He reached up and cupped her neck, drawing her down, possessing her mouth. Whereas he devoured her, wanting to taste, his passion a tidal wave overtaking him, she kissed him hard, demanding more.

But her lips weren't the only thing he wanted to kiss.

"Give me your breasts." She didn't argue, simply shifted that she might offer those perfect globes to him, the puckered nipples in need of attention.

He licked them first, moistening the skin, before he blew on it. Followed by a hard suck. A gentle nip that made her growl, "I am not fragile."

No, she wasn't. She was strong and beautiful, so he bit her, harder this time, pinching her flesh, causing her to cry out.

When he gripped her breasts, he did so tightly, firmly, squeezing then kneading as he worshipped the tips with his mouth. He flipped her onto her back, catching her protest with his mouth.

He wanted better access, so he pinned her legs apart with his body, and as he kissed her, hungrily, he let his fingers tickle up her leg. When he reached the apex of her thighs, he slid his hand over her bare mound.

She shivered. "Touch me," she commanded.

"When I'm ready."

At his refusal to jump to obey, she moaned, opening her mouth for his tongue. As they dueled for supremacy, he let his fingers trail over her to the mouth of her cunt. He rubbed around the petals of her sex, the warm honey making her slick, enough he slid his finger in with ease.

The tightness of her sex, the insides ribbed—for his pleasure—clung to his finger. He knew how it could feel around his cock.

So he teased himself.

He poised himself over her, pressing against her sex, wetting the tip.

Her eyes opened, heavy with passion. Her lips parted and full. "Love me, Jedrek."

The soft plea saw him sinking into her. Balls deep. Seated to the hilt. Filling her up and stretching her.

He shifted his hips, giving it a swirl, and she cried out. Then moaned as he dragged his cock out, the ridges in her channel making him gasp. Only once the tip tickled her lips did he slam back in. Deeply. Again. In and out. The suction of her making him throb. The heat of her making him move faster. And faster.

She matched his quickening pace. He dug his fingers into her ass cheeks, lifting her off the bed, giving himself a better angle to slam his cock.

As the ship they were on growled and groaned, lifting from the planet, he sank deeper.

"Hold on," he said. She reached out and gripped the bed's frame. He held on to her and kept thrusting. The fleshy sound of smacking bodies competed with the roar of the ship. As they penetrated the atmospheric veil, his strokes went long and deep, rubbing over her inner sweet spot.

Gravity fled, and they floated, making his task more difficult.

So he flipped her onto her stomach and spread her legs. "Brace yourself," he ordered. With her holding the wall, he grabbed her by the waist and thrust into her. Drove his cock into her slick cunt and fucked her hard.

She embraced his savage claiming, took each stroke with short pants and hissed, "Yes. Harder. Do it. Bite me."

Bite her? He might have questioned it more but instead found his mouth on the flesh of her shoulder, and before he knew it, he bit down hard.

She screamed as her climax exploded. She quivered around his sheathed cock, fisting him so tight.

Jedrek let out a yell as he ground against her ass. When the gravity came back, his strokes remained hard and fast, triggering her into a second orgasm that finally had him coming, gasping her name.

They collapsed on the bed. Sweaty. Sated. Together.

An alarm sounded.

"What's that?" he asked.

"Well, I couldn't exactly leave openly with you. So, we had to make it look good for my family. As you might recall, I mentioned how my mother drugged you when you fainted—"

"I didn't faint. I was momentarily overcome by your atmosphere."

She snorted. "While you were overcome, Father and I knocked out some city guards, planted evidence you did it. Stole a cruiser and led security forces on an overland chase. Met up with your foster father and then openly blasted off from the planet."

"You did what?" He sat bolt upright in bed.

She leaned back and smiled smugly. "Mother deserved something, so I gave her an abduction to be proud of."

"And started a war?"

She shrugged. "It was the least I could do to make her friends jealous."

With a laugh, he pounced on his princess, his mate, his lover. For now and forever.

EPILOGUE

AFTER THEY SATISFIED each other again, Azteriya leaned into Jedrek, finally realizing that to rely on someone wasn't a weakness. In his presence, she found strength, the kind to throw off a lifetime of chains and to forge her own path.

A path she wouldn't travel alone. She'd found acceptance and the fulfillment of a dream. She'd barely had time to process it, but she'd been asked by Shianny, a mighty female Maez warrior, if she'd like to join their Shield Against Jaqdubwa. A planetary group dedicated to the protection of the sacred forests against the marauding tree-shredding Jaqdubwa who kept trying to invade their groves and tear it down to sell on the Obsidian market.

Her answer, "Will it involve killing things?"

"Much blood and violence."

"I am pregnant."

Shianny gave her an assessing look. "Does that make you an invalid? I gave birth to my eldest on a battlefield and fought with her in a sling on my chest moments after."

Ever felt like you'd found something missing all your life? The Maez were only part of it. Jedrek was the other part, a male who'd given her the one thing she never realized she needed—love.

And even better, his Maez traditions gave her permission to kill to protect it.

———

BEFORE AZTERIYA FINISHED ENACTING her brilliant reverse abduction...

A sleepy-eyed Dorrys stumbled into the garden. A message from Azteriya saying, "Goodbye. I'm eloping with a human," had woken her up. Dorrys knew it was silly to envy her. How exciting she'd found someone.

If only Dorrys could have the same luck.

In the distance, she could hear sirens. She wondered if it had to do with Azteriya's escape.

Sigh. Dorrys sat on a bench and trailed her fingers in the raised pond, faintly smiling as the aquatic creatures within nibbled her fingers. Soon her freedom to do such things would be curtailed.

Maybe I should run away.

But how? And where would she go?

The wail of sirens grew louder as security vehicles swept past. Chasing who?

Thump.

She looked at the far wall and blinked at the giant lizard brandishing a sword in the garden.

"Are you going to kill me?"

It flashed a forked tongue at her.

She stuck her own tongue out right back.

That small act of impertinence was probably why she ended up over his shoulder and abducted.

The End

BUT STAY TUNED because I have a feeling that Dorrys and Clarabelle have a story to tell.

For more Eve Langlais humor and books see EveLanglais.com

Looking for more alien romance?